SoP
(28)

SOMETHING HAPPENED HERE

Norman Levine

VIKING

VIKING
Published by the Penguin Group
Penguin Books Canada Ltd, 10 Alcorn Avenue, Toronto, Ontario,
Canada M4V 1E4
Penguin Books Ltd, 27 Wrights Lane, London WB 5TZ, England
Viking Penguin, a division of Penguin Books USA Inc., 375
Hudson Street, New York, New York 10014, USA
Penguin Books Australia Ltd, Ringwood, Victoria, Australia
Penguin Books (NZ) Ltd, 182-190 Wairau Road, Auckland 10,
New Zealand

Penguin Books Ltd, Registered Offices: Harmondsworth,
Middlesex, England

First published 1991

10 9 8 7 6 5 4 3 2 1

Copyright© Norman Levine, 1991

The following was used by permission:
Excerpted lyrics from "Don't Fence Me In" (Cole Porter) © 1944
Warner Bros. Inc. (Renewed) All rights reserved.

All rights reserved. Without limiting the rights under the
copyright reserved above, no part of this publication may be
reproduced, stored in or introduced into a retrieval system, or
transmitted in any form or by any means (electronic, mechanical,
photocopying, recording or otherwise), without the prior written
permission of both the copyright owner and the above publisher
of this book.

*Publisher's note: This book is a work of fiction. Names, characters, places
and incidents either are the product of the author's imagination or are
used fictitiously, and any resemblance to actual persons living or dead,
events, or locales is entirely coincidental.*

Printed and bound in Canada on acid free paper ♾
by John Deyell Company

Canadian Cataloguing in Publication Data

Levine, Norman, 1923-
  Something happened here

ISBN 0-670-83119-0

I. Title.

PS8523.E87S65 1991   C813'.54   C90-095647-2
PR9199.3.L48565 1991

British Library Cataloguing in Publication Data Available

For Anne

ACKNOWLEDGEMENTS

The stories first appeared in *Encounter*; "CBC
Anthology"; *Saturday Night*; *London Magazine*;
BBC Radio 3; *The Penguin Book of Modern
Canadian Short Stories*; *Quest*; *Woman's Journal*.

They have been published, in translation, in West
Germany (Claassen); Norway (Gyldendal); The
Netherlands (Van Gennep).

Also by Norman Levine

Canada Made Me
One Way Ticket
From a Seaside Town
I Don't Want to Know Anyone Too Well
Selected Stories
Thin Ice
Why Do You Live So Far Away?
Champagne Barn

CONTENTS

SOMETHING
HAPPENED
HERE

BECAUSE OF THE WAR

BECAUSE OF THE WAR

I left Canada in 1949 and went to England because of the eighteen months I lived there during the war. I met my wife because of the war. She was evacuated to Cornwall from London. She also had a weakness for displaced Europeans who had left their country. And I am European — one generation removed. For almost twenty-seven years we were happily married, raised a family, then she became ill and died.

Soon after that the writing stopped. I'd go out in the morning to get the *Times*, do shopping, cook something to eat. Then go for long walks. Or I would sit in the front room, look out of the window, and listen to the wind, the clock, the gulls. The evenings were the most difficult.

After seven months I realized I couldn't go on like this. So I came back to Canada, to Toronto. A city I had never lived in before. I came mid-February (two months before a new book was to be

3

published . . . it was the last thing I read to her in manuscript). I like Canadian winters. But after two weeks in Toronto I didn't want to go out.

I would only leave this room to walk to the corner store and buy two packs of cigarillos. And mail my letters. Then I would go to Ziggy's supermarket. The neat piles of fruit and vegetables. Such lovely colours. And in sizes I wasn't used to. The cheeses from all over. The different bread, bagel, salami, hot dogs — what abundance. Equipped with this I stayed inside, cooked, listened to the radio, made cups of coffee, smoked the cigarillos, and wrote letters to England, Holland, and Switzerland. I like a foreign city. But there was something here that made me uneasy every time I went out.

My publisher had got me this apartment. A large bare room on the seventh floor in the centre of Toronto. It looked shabby from the outside. But one wall was all glass. I watched passenger jets, high-rise office buildings, clusters of bare trees, and some magnificent sunsets. It was even more impressive at night. The lights inside the glass buildings were left on. They made the city look wealthy, full of glitter, like tall passenger liners anchored close together in the dark.

On my first day I went to a bank on Bloor Street to open an account. A small grey-haired woman with glasses came to the counter. "What is your job?"

I told her.

She lowered her head and mumbled.

"Unemployed?"

"No."

As she wrote my name, address, and other particulars, I could see she didn't believe I was in work. I wondered why. I had on a new winter coat. I was wearing a tie, a clean shirt, a dark suit. I had good shoes.

I walked to the Eaton Centre. From the outside it reminded me of Kew Gardens — one greenhouse above another. And seeing people moving sideways on the escalators — like something from "Things to Come."

I had come to get a telephone. And when I came out, with the telephone, I was on a frozen sidestreet. I didn't know where north was. So I asked a woman in a fur coat.

"Don't talk to me," she shouted angrily, waving her hand. "Go away, go away — just walk along — "

I did walk along. The panhandlers kept asking. "Can you spare a quarter?" "Any change sir?" Then told me to have a good day or else to take care. The cold wind blew loose newspapers down Yonge Street. It looked shabby and raw.

But inside it was different.

I'd come in from the cold to this well-heated building. Though the room was warm the air was dry. The toothbrush I left wet at night was like chalk next morning. And when I left out a piece of sliced bread. . . . In the morning I woke to a high-pitched sound. It was the dry bread drying even more.

In those first weeks I went for walks. And discovered a large Chinese section, a Portuguese, Italian,

Polish, Jewish, Greek . . . with their restaurants, bakeries, butchers, bookstores, and banks.

On a cold morning I walked into a district of large houses, wide lawns, a small park. Icicles were hanging from the roofs. And on the lawns the snow had a frozen crust. It was garbage day. The garbage cans, and the tied black-green plastic bags, were on the snow at the edge of the lawns. In the road steam was rising from the manholes.

Because of the ice I was walking slowly through the park when I saw a red bird fly to a young tree. This small red bird in this frozen landscape looked exotic. I was watching this bird when three large dogs appeared. They attacked the garbage cans, ripped the plastic bags, and foraged. They did this, from lawn to frozen lawn, without making a sound. Then went away leaving garbage scattered and exposed.

Some days I gave myself destinations.

One afternoon I decided to walk to the Art Gallery of Ontario. At a busy intersection I had to wait for the lights to change. I looked up and saw a black squirrel on a telephone wire slowly crossing above the crowded street. No one else seemed to take any notice.

Because I saw the squirrel get across and because the sun was shining, I said to the man waiting beside me.

"Isn't this a lovely day?"

"You too," he replied.

Late on a Saturday, I went and bought a paperback of *Heart of Darkness*. Then walked back through fresh snow to the apartment. As the elevator started it began to vibrate. At the top it stopped. The door remained shut. I pressed the number seven button again. It went to the bottom. And stopped. The elevator door still wouldn't open. I tried all the buttons, the switches. Nothing happened except the lights went out. It was then that I realized I was trapped.

I began to call out.

I don't know how long I was there. The air had become stale. I thought: how awkward it will be if I die here. Finally someone did hear me. "OK fellah," I could hear him on the other side. "Don't worry. I'll get the fire department. They will have you out in a matter of minutes." And they did. They forced the door open. I was at the bottom of the shaft. And climbed out into the light and the cold air.

That's how I met Nick, the superintendent of the apartment. He was standing with the firemen. He looked distressed. "Not my fault. I start work yesterday. I no work weekend. Not my fault."

"Of course it's not your fault," I said.

After that Nick and I talked whenever we saw each other. His wife had left him. He had custody of their son. When he left for school in the morning, I watched them wave and smile until the boy finally turned the corner. Nick told me he was Yugoslavian. That he grew up with the Germans in his country. "I see people die. I see people hang. These things I cannot forget.

"I work for the two sisters. They need to fix here plenty. But they no like to spend money."

The two sisters came from France after the war and spoke English with a French accent. They owned the apartment and ran it from an office on the second floor. Every morning — Monday to Friday at ten — I'd go down to see if I had any mail. And be greeted by smiles and good mornings from one of the sisters. "Please sit down. A cup of coffee?"

Edith, the older one, despite her straight grey hair, looked the younger. She was tall, slim, with dark eyes deeply set. She had a long intelligent face. But there was something awkward about her presence. Both sisters were generous, sociable. And both were elegantly dressed.

"These shoes," Edith said, stepping out of one and going easily back into it. "I went to Paris to get them."

"I too go to Paris for my clothes," said Miriam.

She was stocky: blue eyes, black hair, a round face. She smiled a lot and liked to talk. But often when she started to tell a story she would forget the ending and stop in mid-sentence with a startled look.

Edith was separated with two children. Miriam was divorced with two children. They thought I was too much on my own.

"You won't meet people staying in," Miriam said, "or going for walks by yourself. Go to dances. Go to political meetings. Join something —" She forgot what she was going to say. Then in a flat voice said. "In this business you can tell a lot about a person from their luggage."

At the end of March I met Mrs Kronick. She lived on the floor below. A small Jewish woman, seventy-eight, a widow. She came with her husband from Poland after the First World War. He died ten years ago. She had a son, a doctor, in Vancouver. But he rarely came to see her. Mrs Kronick was still a striking woman, very independent. And she looked after herself. Every time I saw her she wore a different hat. But she couldn't tolerate the cold. I was in the lobby, waiting for the elevator, when she walked in from the outside. Her face was pale, her eyes watering.

"It's a Garden of Eden," she said, trying to catch her breath. "A Garden of Eden."

"What have you been doing, Mrs Kronick?"

She was silent. Then quietly said. "Sewing shrouds."

"It's an honour," she added quickly. "Not everyone gets asked."

Next morning Edith knocked on the door of my apartment.

"Did you see what they did in the elevator?"

"No."

"Come, I'll show you."

On the inside of the elevator I saw, scratched on the metal, a badly drawn swastika. And on the inside of the elevator door: *Kill Jews.*

"They don't like us," she said.

Edith's student-daughter told me, "My mother wears dresses from Dior. She has a woman to help her in the house. But she can't throw away a small piece of cheese. She will wrap it up and save it. She also saves brown paper bags that she gets from shopping — to use again. It's because of what happened to her in the war."

Both sisters were delighted with Nick.

"He is so much better than the last one," Miriam said. "He never stops working."

"The last one was too old," said Edith. "He came from the Ukraine. After forty years here — he was still in the Ukraine."

"You must come and meet our friend Henry," Miriam said. "He is very intelligent. Come for brunch next Sunday." And wrote an address and drew a simple map. "Do you think you will be able to find your way?"

"In the war," I said, "I found my way to Leipzig."

On Sunday I took the subway north and travelled as far as it could go. Then began to walk. I had not seen a Canadian spring in thirty years and I had forgotten how colourful the trees were. The flowering crab-apple's pink and crimson; the horse chestnut with its miniature white Christmas trees. And all kinds of maples.

I was walking through a suburb, several cars were beside each house, but no sidewalks.

I walked on the road.

A car drove up, on the opposite side, and stopped. A man got out. He stared at me. Perhaps because I was walking. As I came opposite I called out. "Why didn't they build sidewalks?"

"I'll only be a minute," he said nervously. And ran inside the nearest house.

"This is Hannah," Miriam said.

And I was introduced to a handsome woman in her late fifties: thinning red hair, brown eyes, high cheek-bones, a pleasant face, but there was a certain arrogance. The man opposite was Henry, a professor of Russian at the university. He was wearing jeans and a blue sports shirt. I felt over-dressed in a grey suit. Miriam had on an expensive-looking sack dress in pastel colours. Edith had gone to New York for the weekend. In the other room the table was set.

We were sitting in the adjoining room. A blue Chagall of flowers was on the wall. And faded photographs of young women with attractive faces in old-fashioned clothes.

Henry was around my age. He spoke English with an accent. I told him that he looked very fit.

"I go jogging every morning. I play tennis. I swim. You realize you are the only Canadian here. Hannah comes from Poland. She came just after the war. I came a few years later. What Russian writers do you like?"

"Chekhov and Turgenev."

He smiled. "And what modern ones."

"Babel, Mandelstam, Akhmatova."

"Yes," he said and kept smiling.

I felt my credentials were being examined.

"I have not long come back from Moscow," he said. "The status of a writer in Russia today is determined if he is allowed to visit the West. It is the highest accolade. It is higher than getting your book published."

And I remembered a Russian writer who came to see me in England. He was hitch-hiking. And it was pouring with rain.

"What are you doing?" I asked him.

"Right now. I'm doing an article on suicide in Dostoevsky. Then I will lecture on it."

We went to the other room and sat around the table. In front of each plate there were wine glasses and tall thin glasses with a yellow rose in them.

Miriam came in with a platter of bagel and croissants.

"Don't let them get cold," she called out, "they are delicious."

I sat next to Hannah. She told me she was leaving tomorrow for Israel. "I know a lot of people but I don't like staying with friends or relatives. I will stay in a hotel. My mother told me: Guests and fish stink after three days."

Miriam poured wine into the glasses.

"Why," Hannah asked, "is it so difficult at our age to find another person?"

"Once you have been married," Henry said, "when you meet someone who has also been married, you are both carrying trailers with you. It is this that makes it difficult."

"But people do marry again," Miriam said.

Then Hannah told us how someone she knew got out from Eastern Europe. "He was running across the border when he heard a whistle. He didn't turn around. He kept running. Then he heard the whistle again. He kept running. He expected shots. When he got to the other side he heard the whistle again. And saw it was a bird."

Hannah took a croissant.

"I don't know why," she said, "but people from Europe that I meet in Canada seem to be smaller. I don't mean in size."

"Because in Europe," Henry said, "things are small and intimate, therefore the importance of a person is exaggerated. And over there people talk better."

Miriam brought in ice cream with a hot chocolate sauce. Then waited until she had everyone's attention. "Today," she said with a smile. "I would like us to talk about happiness."

"You cannot generalize about happiness," Henry said. "What is true for one person is not true for another."

"With the truth you can go around the world," Hannah said. "My mother told me that."

"What is happiness for you?" Miriam asked.

"Moments," I said. "You're lucky when they come."

"For me," said Miriam, "it is getting to know another person."

"But Miriam, don't you agree," I said, "that it is impossible, really, to know anyone else at all. At the most it is just speculation."

"It's living with another person," Hannah said. "That's what people can't do without. Once you've had that you want it again."

"On a visit to a mental hospital," I said, "I met a patient. She was in there a long time. She was in there because she was always happy. If someone she liked died, she laughed."

Miriam suddenly stood up. "Such a nice day," she smiled. "Why don't we go for a walk."

So we did, the four of us. We walked on the road in the sunshine. Then Hannah said she had to leave as she had to pack. And Henry became restless. He said to me: "Can I drive you to where you live?"

When he had gone to get the car Miriam said. "Henry must be lonely. He is always the last one to leave a party."

The book came out and the publisher arranged a promotion tour. Everywhere I was taken to be interviewed there was a young rabbi ahead of me. He was being interviewed because he claimed to be "an authority on Death." There was also a singer making the same tour. In Vancouver she said, I love Vancouver. In Calgary, I love Calgary, I love Ottawa, I love Montreal . . . it's beautiful, beautiful. A man from the States said: "I fell in love with Canada. I changed my nationality. I'm going to die here." People were going around saying "I . . . I . . . I . . ." At the end of the week I felt I had given enough radio and TV interviews to satisfy a minor Head of State. But when an article appeared in the *Globe* I had a phone call.

"Do you remember Archie Carter from McGill?"

"Of course," I said, recognizing his voice and seeing a tall man with dark straight hair, thin lips, a sharp nose, a sharp jaw. He used to be an athlete, then something happened, for he had a limp. In our last year at McGill, Archie Carter started a small recording business. He got me to interview visitors as if they were visiting celebrities. Then they would buy the record to take home. In return Archie let me make recordings of the poems of Thomas Hardy.

"Can you come and see me. Or are you busy?"

"Of course I'll come."

"Today?"

"Yes."

He gave me his address.

It brought me to an expensive high rise opposite a grove of young birches. A doorman, his war medals on a pale blue uniform, saluted me.

I pressed the button outside Archie's door. He called out. "Prepare yourself for a shock." "I'm not the same either," I shouted back. When he opened the door I didn't recognize him. He was bald. He had put on weight. All those sharp features were gone. Only his voice was the same. And I wondered what he was seeing in my face.

We shook hands. He led me into a room with a glass wall overlooking the birches. He limped more than I remembered.

"What would you like to drink? I only have Italian wine. But it's a good one."

He came back from the kitchen with two glasses of red wine. We drank in silence.

"I have three daughters," I said. "When they were small a friend from London, a painter, would come to see us once a year. When he arrived he would give the three of them five pounds in separate envelopes. The last time he came he only had two envelopes. He had forgotten the youngest. So he quickly asked me for an envelope and a piece of paper. As I went to get them the youngest ran into another room. I could hear her crying. I thought she was crying because he had forgotten her. So I went in to tell her that people often forget. . . . But the tears were trickling down her face. And she was sobbing. *He's got old. He's got old.*"

"I'm not a failure," Archie said.

"In the end, Archie, we're all failures."

"Oh, I don't know about that. Do you like the wine?"

"Yes."

"I'm in love with Italy," he said. "The food, the climate. Everything. I go there every two years . . . I got this foot in Italy. I was leading my company. A mortar bomb hit me. They had to remove the ankle."

"What happened after McGill?"

"I taught English for a while. Then I began to paint. I'll show you the paintings later." He paused. "Of course I'm mad." And paused again to see what I would say. I said nothing. "When it's bad it's just boring. It was the pain from the wound that brought it on. The first time was in the hospital ship going back from Italy to England. The next time was fifteen years ago."

"What happened —?"

He hesitated. "It's because I have an economic theory that I believe will cure the world's economic problems." He hesitated again and smiled. He had a pleasant smile. "I believe we wouldn't have inflation or unemployment or high prices — things would be more abundant and we would be a lot happier — if people didn't *gyp* one another."

"Did they put you into a mental hospital for that?"

"I went to Lakefield," he said, "before McGill. Some of my friends are ambassadors — people like that — scattered all over. I called up Cairo, Amsterdam, London — and told them about this theory."

"That still doesn't seem bad enough to be put away."

"But I called them at two in the morning. Some of them became concerned and called the police. It was the police who brought me in . . . I thought at this point I was a genius. The hospital I was in was full of people who thought they were geniuses."

He filled the glasses with more wine.

"A nurse in the hospital tried to make me pee. She got a jug full of water and emptied it into an empty jug. So I could see and hear it. She kept repeating this. I still couldn't go. But the other patients, who had been watching, all wet their beds.

"I have invented a word game that I intend to put on the market. I still think I'm not a failure, you know. But I must not forget. I must call this number." And he took out an envelope. And dialled very determinedly. "There is a studio going. And I must get this woman before she lets it to someone else."

He let the phone ring a long time before he hung up.

"What was I saying?"

"What happened after you came out of the hospital?"

"I began to paint. My shrink quite likes them."
He brought several small canvases from his bedroom. They were gentle landscapes of fields and
trees by a river. "What do you think?"

"I like the colours."

"I better phone that woman or else that studio
will go. And I need a studio."

He dialled. No response.

"Remind me to try again."

"Yes," I said.

"It's good you are in Toronto. We have lots to talk
about."

"I'm going to England," I said.

He looked disappointed.

"But I'm coming back."

I got up. "I'll ring when I get back."

"Fine. I better call that woman again."

He took out the envelope. We shook hands. And
I left him dialling the number.

On the way back I saw Mrs Kronick.

"What have you been doing?" I asked.

"I was walking down Yonge Street," she said,
"and I thought of the people I knew who are dead.
What have I done with my life?"

I didn't know what to answer.

"You have a son," I said.

"Yes," she said gently. "That's what I have done
with my life."

The two sisters continued to ask me to small
parties that they arranged for people separated or
divorced. But I met Helen in the supermarket. I

could not find the roasted peanuts in their shells. She was standing near by. I asked her. And she walked over to show me where they were.

She was tall. Light blue eyes, a small fine nose, a small mouth, colour in her cheeks, short blonde hair with a fringe. She smiled easily and had a pleasant voice. Because I detected a trace of an English accent in it I said.

"Where in England are you from?"

"Devon — from Exeter."

"How long have you been here?"

"Thirty-four years."

"I've not long come from England."

The next time I saw her was in a small cemetery. I was coming from my publisher. She was arranging flowers by a stone. "I don't come here often," she said. "It's my husband's birthday."

"Shall we go and have some coffee?"

"My car is here," she said. "Why don't we go home?"

There were oil paintings on the wall, books, and black and white photographs of a handsome-looking man.

"He was a very private person," she said. "It's almost four years. He had come back from a business trip when he had a heart attack."

She made me a cheese and tomato sandwich.

"I met Jimmy during the war. He was with the RCAF. We got married when the war was over and he brought me to Toronto. Then Jimmy's father died. And he had to run the family business. We had a very good marriage for almost thirty years."

Then she told me about her early life in England. How she was brought up by two grandmothers. The one in the city ran a theatre. The other, in the country, was a farmer's wife.

"Why don't you write it down," I said. "It would make a good book."

"I wouldn't know how to go about it."

"Talk into a tape recorder."

"I can talk to you," she said. "Leave me a photograph. That will help."

"No, I'll come up."

That's how it started. Twice a week I would leave the apartment and go there in the late afternoon. She would give me a drink. And talk into the tape. And I would ask her questions and she would answer. Then she would give me dinner. And do another hour of talking into the tape.

One evening there was a thunderstorm.

"Why not stay the night," she said. "There's a bed in the spare room or you can sleep with me."

As I got into bed she said,

"I bruise easily."

Later she said. "I wanted you to know that you had a choice."

Did I have a choice, I wondered.

It was very pleasant having breakfast together. Then walking, in the early morning, down Yonge Street.

After two weeks Helen said, "Why don't you move in here. One room could be your study and where you work."

"I'll have to go to England first and settle things. Then I'll come back."

"The sooner the better," she said.

The two sisters decided to buy a small coffee and cake store for their children. But the children were hardly there. Only Edith and Miriam. And they seemed to be enjoying themselves. As I came in Edith said. "You must have a croissant. They are the best in Toronto. . . ."

"Did you know Nick will be leaving us?"

"No," I said. "But why —"

"He takes too many days off. He doesn't do his work."

Miriam came in. "You're just the person I want to see. We are having a small party on Saturday night. There will be some interesting people. Henry will be there —"

"I have come to say goodbye."

"I don't like goodbyes," said Edith.

"Ella Fitzgerald used to sing," I said:

> *Every time we say goodbye*
> *I die, a little.*
> *Every time we say goodbye*
> *I wonder why, a little.*

"That's Lamartine," Edith said. "*Chaque fois qu'on se dit, au revoir, Je meurs un peu* — Imagine being in a store like this in Toronto and quoting Lamartine.

"I'm sure that in small stores in Toronto — Czechs are quoting from Czech writers, Italians, Hungarians, are doing the same. The Portuguese here are quoting from Portuguese poets —" when I noticed grey airplanes in the sky. I could see them from the store window. They were coming in all directions. I counted a Dakota, six Mustangs with their clipped wings, two Bostons, a Lightning, a Tiger Moth, another Dakota.

"They're airplanes from the Second World War," I said.

"It must be from a museum," Miriam said in her flat voice.

I watched the low-flying planes. They looked so slow. Then they began to circle as if they were going to land.

I went outside to watch the airplanes and saw Nick coming across the car park. He was carrying a loaded shopping bag from the supermarket. I wanted to tell him about the airplanes. But he had his face down. As he came closer I could see tears in his eyes. I thought it was because he had lost his job.

"Tito is dead," he said. And walked by.

The airplanes had disappeared. There was not a trace of their presence. Only a seagull flew low between two high rises.

I was walking by the store that showed the time in the capitals of Europe when I saw Mrs Kronick on her way back to the apartment. She had on a smart black and white suit and a large black hat.

"I'm leaving, Mrs Kronick."

She looked at me for a while. Then said,

"When I leave a person, I don't care if I never see them again."

"But what about those you love?"

"Of course," she said, "with those you love there's always regret."

SOMETHING HAPPENED HERE

SOMETHING HAPPENED HERE

I felt at home soon as I got out of the Paris train and waited for a taxi outside the railway station. I could hear the gulls but I couldn't see them because of the mist. But I could smell the sea. The driver brought me to a hotel along the front. It was a residential hotel beside other residential hotels with the menu in a glass case by the sidewalk. It had four storeys. Its front tall windows, with wooden shutters and small iron balconies, faced the sea. On the ground level was the hotel's dining-room. The front wall was all glass. And there was a man sitting alone by a table.

It looked a comfortable family hotel. The large wooden staircase belonged to an earlier time when it had been a family house. The woman who now owned and ran it liked porcelain. She had cups and saucers on large sideboards, on every landing, as well as grandfather clocks and old clocks without hands. They struck the hour at

27

different times. There were fresh and not so fresh flowers in porcelain vases. There were large mirrors, in wooden frames, tilted against the wall, like paintings. There were china plates, china cups, and china teapots on top of anything that could hold them.

My room on the third floor didn't face the sea but a courtyard. I watched a short man in a chef's hat cutting vegetables into a pot. The room was spacious enough but it seemed over-furnished. It had a large double bed with a carving of two birds on the headboard. A tall wooden closet, a heavy wooden sideboard, a solid table, several chairs, a colour television, and a small fridge fully stocked with wine, brandy, champagne, mineral water and fruit juices. On the fridge was a pad and pencil to mark what one drank.

After I partly unpacked and washed I went down to the dining-room and was shown to a table by the glass wall next to the man sitting alone. He was smoking a cigarette and drinking coffee. He had on a fawn shirt with an open collar and a carefully tied black and white cravat at the neck. He also had fawn coloured trousers. He looked like Erich von Stroheim.

The proprietress came to take my order. She wobbled, coquettishly, on high heels. Medium height, a little plump, in her late forties or early fifties perhaps. She had a sense of style. She wore a different tailored dress every day I was there. A striking person. She had a white complexion and black hair. And looked in fine health. Her teeth were very good. There was a liveliness in her dark eyes. Every time I walked by the desk and the lounge she never seemed far away: doing accounts, dealing with the staff, talking to guests.

I gave her my order in English. I ordered a salad, an omelette, and a glass of *vin rosé*.

When she had gone the man at the next table said in a loud voice,

"Are you English or American?"

"Canadian."

He began to talk in French.

Although I understood some of what he said I replied, "I can't speak French well. I'm *English* Canadian."

"I speak English," he said. "I had lessons in Paris at the Berlitz school. My English teacher, she was a pretty woman, said I was very good because I could use the word barbed-wire in a sentence. My name is Georges."

I told him mine. But for some reason he called me Roman.

"Roman, what do you do?"

"I am a writer."

"Come, join me," he said. "I like very much the work of Somerset Muffin and Heavelin Woof. Are you staying in this hotel?"

"Yes. I arrived a half-hour ago."

"I live in the country. Since my wife is dead I come here once a week to eat. What do you write?"

"Short stories," I said, "novels."

"I read many books — but not novels. I read books of ideas. The conclusion I have come is that you can divide the people of the world. There are

the sedentary. There are the nomads. The sedentary — they are registered. We know about them.
The nomads — they leave no record."

A young waiter, in a white double-breasted
jacket, poured more coffee.

"Do you know Dieppe?"

"No, this is my first time here."

"I will show you."

And he did. When I finished eating he took me
along the promenade. A brisk breeze was blowing
but the sea remained hidden by mist. He brought
me to narrow side-streets, main streets, and
squares. He walked with a sense of urgency. A
short, stocky man, very compact and dapper, with
lively brown eyes and a determined looking head.
He had a bit of a belly and his trousers were
hitched high-up. He carried his valuables in a
brown shoulder bag.

In a street for pedestrians only we were caught
up in a crowd. It was market day. There were shops
on both sides and stalls in the middle.

"Look, Roman, at the *wonderful* colours,"
Georges said loudly of the gladioli, the asters,
lilies, roses, geraniums. Then he admired the
peaches, apricots, butter, tomatoes, carrots, the
heaped strands of garlic and onions. He led me to a
stand that had assorted cheese and large brown
eggs, melons, leeks, and plums. And to another
that had different sausages and salamis. On one
side he showed me live brown and white rabbits
in hutches. And laughed when, directly opposite,
brown and white rabbit skins were for sale. The
street fascinated him. He stopped often and talked

loudly to anyone whose face happened to interest him.

We had a Pernod at a table outside a café that had a mustard and orange facade. He lit a French cigarette. I, a Canadian cigarillo. The pleasure of the first puffs made us both silent. Nearly all the tables were occupied, shoppers were passing, and music came loudly from a record store.

I asked Georges, "What do you think of Madame who runs the hotel?"

"*Très intelligente*," he said and moved his hands slowly to indicate a large bosom. "*Et distinguée*." He moved his hands to his backside to indicate large buttocks. And smiled.

He had a way of talking English which was a lot better, and more amusing, than my French.

He brought me inside an old church. He was relaxed until he faced the altar. He stiffened to attention, slid his left leg forward, as if he was a fencer, and solemnly made the sign of the cross. He remained in that position for several seconds looking like the figurehead at the prow of a ship. When he moved away he relaxed again. And pointed to a small statue of the Virgin with her arms open.

"Roman, the Virgin has opened her legs in welcome."

I was feeling tired when we came out of the church. The train journey, the sightseeing, the conversation . . . but Georges walked on. He was heading for the docks. I said I would go back to the hotel as I had some letters to write.

"Of course," he said, "forgive me. You must be exhausted. Tomorrow, would you like to see where

I live in the country? I will come for you after breakfast."

And he was there, as I came out of the hotel, at eight-thirty, sitting in a light blue Citroen, dressed in the same clothes.

"Did you sleep, Roman?"

"For eight hours."

I could not see the sun because of the mist. But the surf, breaking on the pebbles, glistened. As he drove inland it began to brighten up. He drove fast and well. And he talked continually. Perhaps because he needed someone he could talk English to.

He said he had been an officer in the French navy. That in the last war he had been a naval architect in charge of submarines at their trials.

"I was at Brest, Cherbourg, Toulon, Marseille. My daughter was born when I was stuck in submarine in the mud. My wife told me the nurse came to say, 'The baby she is lovely. But the father — it is dead.' " And he laughed.

On a low hill, ahead, a large institution-like building with many windows and fire escapes.

"Lunatic asylum," Georges said, "full of patriots."

The government, he said, had a publicity campaign for the French to drink more of their wine and appealed to their patriotism. After this whenever he mentioned anyone who liked to drink, Georges called him "a patriot." And if anyone looked more than that, "*Very* patriotic."

The asylum was beside us. A cross on top. And all the top windows barred.

"When I was a boy . . . this place made big impression. Before a storm . . . the wind is blowing . . . and the people in lunatic asylum scream. I will never forget."

He drove through empty villages, small towns. He stopped, walked me around, and did some shopping. I noticed that the elaborate war memorials, by the churches, were for the 1914-1918 war. The only acknowledgement of the Second World War was the occasional stone, suddenly appearing in the countryside, at the side of the road, that said three or four members of the Resistance had been shot at this spot.

"I have been to America," Georges said. "I like the Americans. But sometimes they are infantile. Nixon — dustbin. Carter — dustbin."

He drove up a turning road by a small, broken, stone bridge that had rocks and uprooted trees on either side. "There is a plateau," he said, "high up. It has many meadows. The water gathers there for many rivers. Once in a hundred years the water very quickly goes down from the plateau to the valley and turns over houses, bridges, trees. Last September a priest on the plateau telephone the Mayor and say the water looks dangerous. But the Mayor, a young man, say it is only an old man talking. Half-hour later the water come down and drown thirty people and took many houses. It was Sunday so many people were away from the houses otherwise more drown. All happen last September. In a half-hour. But it will not happen for another hundred years. And no one will be here who knows it. The young won't listen. They will, after some years, build houses in the same place. And it will happen all over again."

In one of the large towns he stopped and showed me the cemetery where his family is buried. It was a vault, all stone, no grass around. Nor did any of the others have grass anywhere. On the stone was a vertical tablet with two rows of de Rostaings. The first was born in 1799. "He was town architect." A few names down. "He had lace factory. . . . He build roads. . . . See how the names become larger as we come nearer today."

"Will you be buried here?"

"No. My wife is Parisian. She is buried in Paris. I will lie with her."

He continued on the main road, then turned off and drove on a dirt road. Then went slowly up a rough slope until he stopped, on the level, by the side of a converted farmhouse.

"We are here," he said.

We were on a height. Below were trees and small fields — different shades of green, yellow and brown. Instead of fences or hedgerows, the fields had their borders in trees. And from this height the trees gave the landscape a 3-D look.

Georges introduced me to Marie-Jo, a fifteen-year-old schoolgirl from the next farm who did the cooking and cleaning during the summer. Short blonde hair, blue eyes, an easy smile. She was shy and tall for her age and walked with a slightly rounded back. While Marie-Jo barbecued salmon steaks at the far end of the porch, under an over-hanging chimney, Georges walked me around. In front of the house, under a large elm, was a white table and white chairs. It was quiet. A light wind on the small leaves of the two near poplars. "They say it will rain," he said. And beside them a border of roses, geraniums, and lobelia.

We ate outside on a white tablecloth. I could hear people talking from the farm below. Further away someone was burning wood. The white smoke rose and thinned as it drifted slowly up. On top of the house was a small stone cross. A larger metal cross was embedded in the concrete of the front fence.

"I am Catholic," Georges said. "There are Protes-tants here too. My sister married a Jew. A Pole. From Bialystok."

Marie-Jo brought a round wooden board with cow and goat cheeses on it. And Georges filled my glass with more red wine.

"When I was young boy of seven we had great distilleries in my country. We hear the Russians are coming. We wait in the street. It is beginning to snow. But I do not want to go home. Many people wait for the Russians.

"Then they come. They look giants with fur hats and big boots and long overcoats. *Very* impressive.

"After a while — what happens? First the women. They say to Russian soldiers — you want drink? They give them drink. A little later, in the street, you see the women wearing the Russian furs for —"

Georges indicated with his hands.

"Muffs," I said.

"Yes, muffs, muffs. The women all have muffs.

"Then the French men give drink. Later, the French men you see in the street — they are wearing the Russian boots.

"The peasants — they *drowned* the Russians."

Marie-Jo brought ripe peaches, large peaches, lovely colours, dark and light, red to crimson. They were juicy and delicious.

"How did your sister meet her husband?"

"At the Sorbonne. My sister always joking. He serious. I did not think they would stay together. When she go to Poland to meet his family we are worried. We Catholic. They Jew. They have two children. Then the war. The Nazis. He is taken away. My mother, a tough woman, get priest and doctor to make fake certificate — say the two boys baptized. But my mother did not think that was enough. She tell me to take the boys to a farmer she know in the Auvergne. I take them. When I meet the farmer I begin to tell story. But the farmer just shake my hand. Say nothing. The children stay with him for the war."

"What happened to the Polish Jew?"

"He died."

We went to have coffee in the barn. The main room of the house. High ceiling with large windows and the original beams. To get to it from the inside you would go up some stairs. But you could walk to it from the garden by going up a grass slope. "All farmers have this for the cattle to go up and down," Georges said.

It was also his studio. On the walls were oil
paintings by his uncle who was dead. Impression-
ist paintings of the landscape around here. "They
sell for 40,000 francs," Georges said. "I have about
thirty good ones. Some in the flat in Paris, some in
the flat in Cannes. A few here." He also had his
own paintings — on the wall, and one on an easel
— like his uncle's but not as good.

Marie-Jo appeared with a jug full of coffee.

"I am working on book," he said. "I have contract with Paris publisher. Eleven years — I am not
finished. It will be traveller's dictionary of every
place in world that someone has written."

We had coffee. He lit a cigarette and went over to
his record player.

"Roman — have you heard the Japanese Noh?"

I answered no with a movement of my face.

"Very strange. Sounds like a cat . . . and a chain
with bucket . . . and a man flogging his wife. I was
twenty, a midshipman on cruiser. We visit Japan.
Suddenly I was put there, for six hours, listening to
this."

He put a record on. "This is the cat . . ." a single
note vibrated . . . "looking for another cat . . ."
Georges was standing, talking with gestures.
"Now, the long chain with a bucket going down
well . . . it needs oil. . . . This is a man flogging his
wife. . . ."

He stopped the record.

"The Japanese they are different from the
French. They believe the dead are with us all the
time."

He showed me a photograph of his wife, Colette.

She looked a determined woman, in her late forties. A strong jaw, thin lips, blonde hair pulled back on her head, light eyes.

"She had beautiful voice," Georges said. "One of the things I like in people is the voice. If they have bad voice it is difficult for me to stay long with them."

"How long is it since she died?"

"Three years."

He must have thought of something else for he said abruptly, "If you do not come into the world — then you cannot go."

He took me for a walk through the countryside. There were all kinds of wild flowers I didn't know and butterflies and some, like the small black and white, I had not seen before either. But it was the trees that dominated. And I like trees. Probably because I have lived so long in Cornwall facing stone streets and stone terraces.

I wondered why Georges was not curious about my past. He appeared not interested in my personal life. Though I did give him bits of information.

"How long will you be in Dieppe?"

"Two, maybe three days more," I said. "I want to go to England, to a flat I have in Cornwall, and do some work."

It was after nine, but still light, when we got back to Dieppe. "I know a small place but good," Georges said. And brought me to a restaurant opposite the docks called L'Espérance.

We were both tired and for a while didn't talk. I ordered marinated mackerel, a salad, and some chicken. And Georges ordered a half-melon, veal, and cheese. Also coffee and a bottle of red wine.

Two tables away a man and a woman, both plump, in their late fifties or early sixties, were eating with relish. The woman had a large whole tongue on her plate to start with, the man a tureen of soup. He tucked his napkin into his open-neck shirt. Then they both had fish, then meat with potatoes, then cheese, then a large dessert with whipped cream on top. . . . And all the time they were eating they didn't speak.

Beside them, going away towards the centre of the restaurant, were two young men. They were deaf and dumb. They were talking with their hands. They also mimed. When they saw us looking they included us in their conversation. One of the men looked Moroccan, with a black moustache on the top lip and down the side of his face. He was lean. And he mimed very quickly and well. He pointed at Georges' cigarette and at my cigarillo. And shook his head. He touched his chest and pretended he was coughing. And shook his head. He then showed himself swimming, the breast stroke. He was smiling. He showed us that he was also a long distance walker, getting up and staying in one place, he moved heel and toe, heel and toe, and that curious rotation of the hips.

"Roman," Georges said loudly. "The woman you see is fat. Her husband is fat. Look how they eat. Beside them two men, slim, young. They have to talk with their hands. They look happy — all the time the food comes — they are talking. But the two beside them — they do not talk at all — they concentrate on next bite. If I had movie camera — that is all you need. No words. No explanation. If I was young man, Roman, I would make films."

As he drove me to the hotel, Georges could not forget the scene in the restaurant. On the hotel's front door there was a sign saying it was full.

"Tomorrow," Georges said, "I no see you."

As tomorrow was Sunday I asked him if he was going to church.

"No, I do not like the clergy. The elm tree need spray. They get disease. I know a young man. He will do it. But I have to get him. And I go to see an old friend. He was officer with me. He now alone in Rouen. We eat lunch on Sunday when I am here. Two old men. I see you the day after."

And we shook hands.

Next morning, I opened the large window of the room. The sun was out. It was warm. A blue sky. After breakfast I decided to go for a walk. I crossed the harbour by an iron bridge. And went up a steep narrow street of close-packed terraced houses. It looked working class. The houses were small, drab, unpainted. And the sidewalks were narrow and in need of repair. They had red and pink geranium petals that had fallen from the window boxes on the small balconies.

I passed an upright concrete church with a rounded top. It stood by itself, stark, against the skyline. I went through tall undergrowth and, when clear of it, I saw I was on top of cliffs. They were an impressive sight: white-grey, sheer, and at the bottom pebbles with the sea coming in.

I walked along for about an hour, on top of the cliffs, when I noticed the path becoming wider as it started to slope down. The cliffs here went back from the sea and left a small pebbled beach. People were on it.

I was looking at the dirt path, as I walked down, because it was uneven and steep when I saw a shrew, about two inches long, over another shrew lying on its side. The one on its side was flattened as if a roller had gone over it. I watched the head of the live shrew over the belly of the dead one — there didn't seem to be any movement. Then, for no reason, I whistled. The live shrew darted into the grass. And I saw the open half-eaten belly of the one on its side, a brilliant crimson. The colour was brighter than any meat I had seen at the butchers.

The small beach wasn't crowded. The surf gentle . . . the water sparkled . . . a family was playing boules. Someone was wind surfing across the length of the beach . . . going one way then turning the sail to go the other, and often falling in. A man in a T-shirt brought a dog, a terrier, on a leash. Then he let him go into the shallows. Under an umbrella a young woman was breast-feeding a baby. Nearer to the water a tall woman with white skin and red hair was lying on her back, topless. People were changing using large coloured towels . . . while the continual sound of the low surf as it came in breaking over the pebbles and sliding back.

I had brought a picnic: bread, a hard-boiled egg, cheese, tomatoes, a pear. And a can of cider to wash it down. After I had eaten I took off my shirt, shoes, socks, and lay down on the stones.

A loud noise woke me. It was two boys running over the stones between my head and the cliffs. I sat up. I didn't know how long I had been asleep. The surface of the water sparkled. The click of the boules was still going. From somewhere a dog was barking. The cliffs, a few yards behind me and on both sides, had light green streaks in the massive white grey. And high up, on the very top, a thin layer of grass.

The tide was coming in. I put on shirt, socks, and shoes, and walked over the pebbles to a paved slope that led from the beach to the road. I could now see a narrow opening between the cliffs. And as I walked up the slope the opening fanned out to show a suburb of houses with gardens, green lawns, and trees. As I came to the top of the paved slope I saw, across the road, on a stone, in French and English.

On this beach
Officers and Men of the
Royal Regiment of Canada
Died at Dawn 19 August 1942
Striving to Reach the Heights Beyond

You who are alive on this beach
remember that these men died far from home
that others here and everywhere might freely
enjoy life in God's mercy.

When I got back to the hotel the "full" sign had been taken down. Madame greeted me with a smile.

"You have caught the sun. I have surprise for you."

She soon re-appeared with a thin blonde girl of about twelve or thirteen.

"This is Jean. She is from Canada," Madame said proudly. "From Alberta."

"Where from in Alberta?" I asked.

"Edmonton," the girl replied in a quiet voice.

"How long will you be in Dieppe?"

"I live here. I go to school."

"When were you in Edmonton?"

"Three weeks ago."

"Is your father there?"

"No, he is somewhere else. He travels. I'm with my mother."

"Can you speak French as well as you can English?"

"I can speak it better," she said.

And she was glad to go off with Madame's only daughter, who was older and not as pretty, to roller-skate on the promenade.

"She is charming," Madame said as we watched both girls run to get out.

"I went for a walk today, Madame," I said, "and came to the beach where in the war the Canadians —"

"*Ah.*" She interrupted and shook her head, then raised an arm, in distress or disbelief. She tried to find words — but couldn't.

"I have read many books about it," she said quickly. "Do you want to see the cemetery?"

"No," I said.

That evening, while in the dining-room, I decided to leave tomorrow. For over three weeks I had been travelling in France. All inland, until Dieppe. It had been a fine holiday. I had not been to France before. But now I wanted to get back to the familiar. I was also impatient to get back to work. I had brought with me a large notebook but I had written nothing in it.

I said to Madame at the desk, "I will be leaving tomorrow. Could you have my bill ready?"

"Of course," she said, "you will have it when you come down for breakfast."

"It is a very comfortable hotel. Are you open all year?"

"In December we close."

"Has it been a good season?"

"I think I go bankrupt," she said loudly. "Oil — up three times in two months. It is impossible to go on —" She held up a sheaf of bills.

"I will tell my friends," I said.

"Is kind of you," she said quietly. And gave me several brochures that said the hotel would be running a weekly cookery course in January and February of next year.

Late next morning, with my two cases in the lounge, I was having a coffee and smoking a cigarillo, when Georges appeared. He saw the cases.

"Yes," I said. "I'm going today."

"What time is your boat?"

"It goes in an hour."

"I will take you."

He insisted on carrying the cases to his car. Madame came hurrying away from people at the desk to shake my hand vigorously and hoped she would see me again.

While Georges was driving he gave me a card with his address in the country, in Cannes, and in Paris. And the dates he would be there. Then he gave me a large brown envelope. I took out what was in it — a small watercolour of Dieppe that he had painted. It showed the mustard and orange café with people sitting at the outside tables and others walking by. On the back he had written, "For Roman, my new friend, Georges."

"When I get to England," I said, "I will send you one of my books."

"Thank you. I should like to improve my English. Perhaps I find in it something for my traveller's dictionary."

At the ferry I persuaded Georges not to wait.

"Roman, I do not kiss the men."

We shook hands.

I sat in a seat on deck, at the stern, facing Dieppe. The ferry turned slowly and I saw Dieppe turn as well. The vertical church with the rounded top, the cathedral, the square, the houses with the tall windows, and wooden shutters, and small iron balconies.

Then the ferry straightened out and we were in the open sea. After a while it altered course. And there were the cliffs where I had walked yesterday and the narrow opening. I kept watching the cliffs and the opening. And thought how scared they must have been coming in from the sea and seeing this.

The sun was warm, the sea calm. And when I next looked at the cliffs the opening had disappeared. All that was there was the white-grey stone sticking up. I thought of gravestones . . . close together on a slope. . . . You could see nothing else. Just gravestones. And they were gravestones with nothing on them . . . they were all blank.

On the loudspeaker the captain's voice said that coming up on the left was one of the world's largest tankers. People hurried to the rails with their cameras.

I went down to a lower deck and stood in the queue for the duty free.

GIFTS

GIFTS

Late November 1979 I flew to Canada to give three
lectures and readings. In Toronto and Montreal I
would talk at universities. In Ottawa — where I
was to start — I would give a reading to the blind.
A light snow was falling as the taxi went through
heavy afternoon traffic to the Château Laurier. I
was shown into a large, comfortable room, on the
second floor, newly furnished, with a double bed,
easy chairs, a writing desk, telephone, colour television. From the window I could see the Peace
Tower, not far away, hear the chimes on the quarter
hour. In the other room, bright from the fluores-
cent lights, the bath was long with no taps, just a
metal wheel that I could turn for hot or cold. I
flicked a switch by the television, soft music came
in both rooms.

After the bath I felt refreshed. I rang an old
girlfriend. She wasn't in. I rang my mother.

"Where are you?"

"At the Château Laurier."

What are you doing in the Château Laurier?"

"They have put me up here."

"How much is the room?"

"I don't know — I'm not paying. See you in half an hour."

"Yes," she said. "When you come you'll have something to eat."

No matter how many times I have told my mother that I now earn a living from my work and I can travel where I want to, whenever I'm in Ottawa and go to see her, she is convinced that I have no money and that I'm hungry.

I walked across Confederation Square in the fading light feeling cheerful. In the window of Books Canada there was a poster about the reading to the blind. I went down Elgin to Laurier, crossed the canal by the bridge, down Nicholas to Rideau . . . and realized I was following the route my father used to take with the horse and wagon.

There were now, of course, no horses and wagons. And there were other changes. But the slowness, the small-town atmosphere of this part, was the same.

I took a shortcut by Rideau Flowers and came out, opposite the little park, to the senior citizen building. I rang the bell, the downstairs door buzzed. She was waiting at the open door of her apartment.

"You look well," I said and kissed her.

"I feel much better than a couple of months ago."

The small apartment was very warm. The table in the living room was set with all the courses laid out for me: orange juice, salad, marinated herring, gefilte fish, chicken with potatoes and carrots, and apple compote.

"Sit down," she said. "You eat — I'll talk.

"I went to see the doctor last week for a checkup. He tells me I'm in good condition. Good condition. How can I be in good condition, doctor, when I've had seven operations?

" 'For a woman your age you are in good condition.' Then he says, 'I'm not saying tomorrow or next week but did you think of going into a nursing home?' This upset me. 'Doctor,' I told him, 'as long as I don't burn my dinner and I don't have to run with my water to the bathroom every few minutes — why should I go to a nursing home?'

" 'That's the time to go to a nursing home,' he said, 'when you can enjoy it. There is no shopping, no cooking, no cleaning. You come and go as you like.'

"He made going into a nursing home sound like going to Florida. The gefilte fish —"

"It's delicious," I said.

" — I no longer make it. It's from a tin. Do you want another piece?"

"I don't know if I can eat all this."

She had lost weight since my last visit. It suited her. The flesh, on the under part of the arms, was hanging loose. But the alert expression in her pale face, the large blue eyes, were the same.

"In the last war," she said, "you were in the air force. If you were in the last war then the government will give you a job here."

"Doing what?"

"Being a commissionaire at one of the government buildings."

I thought I might as well go along with her.

"But there must be a lot of people still alive from the last war," I said. "How can the government give every one a job as a commissionaire?"

"They work shifts," she said.

She went to the kitchen and came back with a large cup of hot coffee. I listened as she told me how they put the pacemaker in: "It saved my life." How she fell and broke some ribs: "That was a killer." All the while she talked about her ailments, I thought how independent she was and spirited and self-contained.

"When I'm in hospital I try to get on my legs. And I walk up and down in the room. Then I get better."

She caught sight of herself in the wall mirror and, a bit of vanity, casually smoothed her thinning white hair.

"No one in my family has lived this long."

"Do you see many people?"

"When I go for a walk . . . or in the park. I don't have people come here anymore. It means I've got to cook. And the talking wears me out. I watch television, I read the paper, and I have the telephone. Sometimes I get lonesome — and feel sorry for myself. Then I take a bus to a shopping centre. Not to get anything. Just to see people enjoying themselves . . . buying things, looking at the merchandise, the money changing hands. I like all this. Years ago, Pa and I should have got a little business. I know I would have made a success —"

I looked at my watch. I had to go back to the Château for an interview. A reporter from *The Citizen* was going to be there in fifteen minutes. I told this to my mother.

"I enjoyed this visit," I said. "Thanks for the meal." And stood up to put on my coat.

"It's a pleasure to talk to someone you know."

She tried to give me a five-dollar bill.

"Mother, I should be giving you money."

At the door she opened her purse and took out a handful of change and insisted that I take it. "You can always use a few quarters and dimes."

When I came out of the building I looked back. She was at the window waving.

A young man with pink cheeks and a black straggly beard was sitting at a table by the wall drinking a cup of coffee. He had two of my books beside him.

"I'm sorry I'm late."

While I was answering his questions and he was writing in his notebook I noticed two young men and a girl sitting at the table opposite. They were finishing their supper. They kept glancing in my direction. After the reporter left, and I was on my second cup of coffee and a cigarillo, one of the young men walked over. He said my name.

"Yes," I said.

"We like your stories. May we come and join you?"

"Of course," I said. "Are you staying at the Château?"

"We're on the third floor."

"I'm on the second. Where are you from?"

"Toronto."

"I'm going there the day after tomorrow."

They were youthfully attractive. And appeared uneasy . . . perhaps they were shy. The girl was called Julie. She was very compact in her smallness — alert dark eyes, dark hair, small nose, small mouth. She had a look of slight surprise on her face. She told me she wrote poetry and had some poems in *The Canadian Forum*. The taller of the two men, with a head of dark wavy hair, was called Frank. He had conventional good looks and wore white corduroy trousers and a black roll-neck sweater. The stockier one, Jim, had brown curly hair, a wide face, in jeans and denim windbreaker over a blue T-shirt. They were students.

"I read in the paper," Frank said, "that you are coming back to live here."

"Yes, in the spring."

He looked disappointed.

"After what you wrote, I didn't think you would want to come back."

"Circumstances change," I said.

"But what made you leave is still here," Jim insisted. "If anything it has got worse."

I listened while they told me how provincial the life still was . . . that the centre of a community was the supermarket . . . that people's attitudes were

"There must be something in it for me." And that the country remained on the edge of the map — "things happen somewhere else."

"It just isn't good enough," Jim said.

"It's a lot better than it was," I said.

"Maybe. But it still isn't good enough. We only have one life and I don't see why we have to live it out here."

They didn't look like social misfits. And I could tell they came from people with money. They had another year at university but they couldn't wait to get away.

"What do you need a university education for?" Julie asked.

"For when you're in solitary," I replied.

By the time I finished another cup of coffee, I realized that Julie was with Frank, and Jim was a friend. And the sort of society they wanted was something between socialism and utopia.

Changing the subject, Julie said, "I have only read a few of your stories in magazines. I like the way you describe the small details of everyday life. But if I may make one criticism — you don't make use of fantasy. If you could have fantasy in your stories then you would reach a wider audience."

I wasn't going to try and explain the complicated way I go about writing anything.

"You may be right," I said.

"Look at Isaac Bashevis Singer," she said. "He believes in the afterlife, in demons, goblins — God."

"I'm not a believer," I said. I suddenly felt tired.

"If you will excuse me, I have to get up early for an interview."

"Perhaps we will see you at breakfast," Julie said and smiled.

"Yes," I said.

They were not there for breakfast. But I didn't linger as I had to go to the sixth floor to the radio studios. And from there a car was waiting to take me to the outskirts of Ottawa for a TV interview. I came back after lunch to the room to go over the parts I would read from my books. At three-thirty, as I still had a half-hour, I thought I would walk to the institute. It was a cold, bright sunny day. As I came near the place, in a residential area, I could see men and women in winter coats walking in the same direction and hear the tapping of the white sticks.

The lounge, where I was to read, was full of light. A table, at the far wall, had coffee on a burner. There were white cups standing in saucers and some biscuits and a cake. People kept coming in, some had dark glasses. They stood, quietly, against the walls. Others felt their way to the chairs that were in irregular semicircles. The sun was coming through the windows and onto the sides of some of the faces but they didn't seem to be aware of this. A middle-aged attractive woman came in elegantly dressed in a red suit. She stood by the table at the back and smiled in my direction.

There was no introduction. I began by saying that I grew up in Ottawa, in Lower Town. And this was the Ottawa I grew up in. . . .

Not a sound, all the time I read. And when I finished there was silence.

I continued by saying I went to university in Montreal, to McGill, and read them a bit about that.

Still no sound.

I noticed that some had their clothes on awkwardly. I could see the white bloomers of an elderly lady. She was sitting beside an elderly man. They were holding hands.

I asked if anyone had questions.

No one spoke.

I told them that after McGill I left Canada and went to live in England. And read descriptions of St Ives: the bay in summer and during a storm . . . seeing rainbows . . . the white-yellow sand beaches . . . how it looked when the tide was in and what you could see when the tide was out . . . the harbour with Cornish and French fishing boats and gulls . . . the moors with gorse, bracken and granite boulders. And the small green fields with hedgerows full of wild flowers.

I asked again if there were any questions.

A thin woman, with glasses and white hair, sitting very erect, said quietly, "I like your descriptions."

A tall man with dark glasses, standing against the wall, said in a stronger voice, "We prefer when you describe things to dialogue."

I then read a description of the sun coming up on the prairies, of a snowstorm in downtown Montreal, of spiderwebs in a garden after a rain.

I had read for almost an hour. They still seemed reluctant to talk. I thought I would stop.

The attractive woman in the red suit thanked me for coming. And said John was now going to give me a cup of coffee.

A young man in a white shirt, a resident, left his chair and felt his way to the table at the back. I watched as he poured the coffee and began to walk slowly in my direction. I was talking louder than usual to someone near me (he said he had a tape recorder for Christmas and he had recorded my reading) when I saw John stumble and fall. He picked himself up, someone else picked up the cup and saucer, and went back to the table. I walked over. He poured coffee in again. I took it from him with a piece of cake and thanked him.

They began, quietly and hesitantly, to talk among themselves. Then they left their chairs, and the wall, and came up to me. A bald old man said, "I saw a rainbow once. I was on a lake, near Ottawa. I was ten." A plump, short lady dressed in green said she remembered Lower Town from what I read. She grew up on St Patrick Street. Someone else said they remembered winter with icicles and being pulled in a sleigh by a dog. The attractive woman who thanked me moved closer. "I hope you don't get the wrong idea," she smiled. "But it is only when I stand this close that I can see you at all, and then only fuzzy." She hoped that now that I had come perhaps other writers would come and read to them. And told me that most of the audience were people who lived at home —

there weren't that many residents — and that not everyone was completely blind.

A young woman came up and asked if she could run her hands over my face.

When I came out I was glad to be outside. I walked very briskly a few blocks. Then stopped. And stood there. Staring at the sky, the bare trees — what lovely colours — a bird on a wire, a young grey cat on a verandah, a black squirrel crossing the road. I just stood there and looked and looked. . . .

When I got back to the Château Laurier there was a note from Julie that said could I come up and see them in Room 320.

I did go up. They were very relaxed with two bottles of champagne on the desk and all kinds of delicatessen food around them. "Glad you could join us," Frank said. And Julie produced an extra glass. Frank had a copy of *The Citizen*.

"You're on page five —"

There was the interview, over two columns, with a photograph taken four years earlier.

" — and we're on page one."

I couldn't see anything that might refer to them. He pointed to a small notice — two sentences — a branch of the Bank of Montreal was robbed by a man and he got away with an undisclosed sum of money.

Nothing, I thought, surprises me any more.

"Why did you do it?" I asked.

"It's something we have been thinking about for a while. We wanted to see if we could do it. Jim worked in a bank — so he knew how — all he needed was a uniform and to go there before it opened."

"Did you have a gun?"

"Yes."

"Bullets?"

"Yes."

"Would you have used them?"

"I don't know," Jim said. "We didn't have to."

I thought, was this bravado or was there something unstable? And why did they tell me?

Julie poured more champagne and I had smoked meat and a pickle.

"What are you going to do with the money?"

Silence.

Frank finally said, "You are going to Toronto for your next lecture."

"Yes."

"So are we. It would be an honour if we could drive you there."

"Thanks," I said. "It's very good of you."

"Could you be in the lobby and ready to leave at 3 A.M.?"

"Are you going to rob another bank?"

They found that amusing.

They were waiting in the lobby with their luggage when I came down. Outside, in the dark, it was cold. I sat with Jim in the back. Frank was driving, Julie was beside him. They didn't appear tired. But I could hardly keep my eyes open. On the car radio a woman was singing *Weekend in Canada*. The streets were empty and Frank was driving fast.

"You drive very well," I said.

"I thought at one time of being a racing driver. But I knew I didn't have the dedication."

When we got out of Ottawa they appeared even more at ease. Gone was that vague discontent that was there when I met them. They began to sing a mixture of revolutionary and popular songs: *Joe Hill, John Brown's Body, Ode to Joy, Kevin Barry,* as well as John Denver songs that I knew and the Beatles. I didn't join in. Although I sing when I'm by myself, friends have told me I can't carry a tune. In any case I felt too warm even with the window open.

I must have fallen asleep because when I woke up the car had stopped. We were in a small town, or village, on the main street. Not a soul was outside.

"Where are we?"

"About halfway," Frank said. "Have a good sleep?"

"I think so."

"You were snoring," Julie said.

A light snow. I could see the flakes by the streetlight. Everything looked shut and quiet.

"Why have we stopped?"

"Would you like to help us?"

"What is it you want me to do?"

Jim took out a leather case and opened it. He handed four bundles of twenty-dollar bills to each of us. "You and Julie do the side streets on that side. We'll do the side streets on this. Then we'll both do the opposite sides of the main. Put two twenty-dollar bills in each door. Not the stores. Only the houses."

For the next fifteen minutes or so I walked briskly to the front doors of houses and pushed through the letter slots two twenty-dollar bills. I no longer felt tired or sleepy. At only one house was there a moment of anxiety when a small dog barked. But no lights came on and no one came to the door. Otherwise we moved from house to house, street to street . . . the snow falling . . . coming back for more bundles — until there were no more.

When it was over, and we all were in the car, there was a shared sense of excitement as if we had taken part in a forbidden pleasure. Julie suddenly kissed the three of us. "Money makes a girl passionate."

Jim said: "I kept these back as souvenirs." And gave two twenty-dollar bills to each of us, including himself. They were crisp notes and I put mine in my back buttoned-down pocket.

"I'd give anything, "Frank said, "to see some of the faces when they go to the door this morning."

The ploughs, the small trucks, were attacking the fallen snow when we arrived in Toronto. It was like a small army. The university had reserved a room in the Windsor Arms. When we got there it was time to go our separate ways.

"You're famous," Julie said looking affectionately into my eyes. "I thought famous people were different."

I shook hands with Frank and Jim.

Julie gave me a prolonged kiss.

"I'll read all your books," she said.

"And I'll look in the paper to see what banks have been robbed."

At the lecture I talked about the past confronting the present and what matters are moments. And gave examples from my stories. Afterward there was a small party at a professor's house. I got back to the hotel after midnight.

Next morning I caught a taxi early as I had to get the morning train to Montreal. The taxi driver spoke English with a heavy accent. I asked him where he was from.

"Israel," he said.

Outside Union Station the driver brought my case from the back. I asked him how much. He said four dollars. I put my hand in my pocket and drew out one of the twenty-dollar bills.

"I can't change that," he said. "I have just started. Where would I get money to change that?"

"Make it ten dollars," I said.

He began, slowly, to take out crumpled one-dollar bills and crumpled two-dollar bills, from different pockets, and placed them into my open hand.

To pass the time, and to apologize for the much too large tip, I said, "It's only money."

He looked startled, then angry.

"What do you mean it's only money. Why do you think I get up when it is still dark and cold — to drive through these streets. Only money." He began to shout hysterically. "I have to work long hours, nights too, and weekends. For what am I doing this? Tell me?"

I walked away . . . aware that I'd stumbled on a simple truth, if there is such a thing. While he continued shouting and waving his hands so that people walking by looked in wonder as to what was wrong between us.

On another occasion, seventeen years earlier, in December 1962, when the children were still small (10, 8, 6), we were living in St Ives, Cornwall, in a large old terraced house that I rented from a widow at twelve pounds a month. I only had a few books published then and was behind with the rent. I was writing mostly short stories as a way of earning money and at the same time trying to get on with a new novel. The weeks before Christmas were an anxious time. It seemed that I was always waiting for a cheque. This time was no exception. I had sent a new story to *Harper's Bazaar*. They had accepted it on December 7 for their top price of twenty-five guineas. And I was watching every postal delivery. Meanwhile I had to tell the milk-man that he would be paid next week, the same with the baker, and the groceries from the Co-op. As the days passed the children began to make decorations and paper chains and cards. But my wife began to worry, how were we going to get through with so little money. We got by with beans on toast, cheese on toast, and macaroni with cheese.

A week later I went, with the little change I had, to the public phone box at the top of the cemetery and called up *Harper's Bazaar* hoping I would get the literary editor. She assured me the cheque was on its way. And could I send her another story in the spring.

But three days later the cheque still hadn't arrived. I was up here, in the attic room, wondering what to do when Martha, our eldest, came running up the stairs shouting. "Dad. Dad. Look what the postman left — smoked salmon."

She gave me this long, neatly wrapped parcel with white, stiff cardboard on the outside. In the top left-hand corner a label said: "Nolan, fishmonger, Dublin." And there was my name and address and in large letters "Smoked Salmon — Perishable."

I quickly brought it down to the kitchen.

My wife and kids watched me unwrap it.

It was the largest smoked salmon I had seen.

"Who sent it?" my wife said happily.

I looked through the parcel.

"It doesn't say. They forgot to put it in."

I sliced large slices, very thin. And we ate them with brown bread, cut lemon, and pepper from the small pepper mill.

We had smoked salmon for lunch and smoked salmon for dinner and, next day, smoked salmon for breakfast.

It was too large for our small fridge so we kept it where it was cold — between the outside front door and the inner door. And had to take it away when the milkman called, the baker, and the grocer.

It seemed such a luxury (the whole family at the kitchen table, eating platefuls of smoked salmon) when there was hardly any food in the house.

At night in bed we couldn't sleep.

"Who do you think sent it?'

"I don't know."

"It's from Dublin — you don't think Edna?"

"No," I said.

"I hope not," my wife said.

"Perhaps it was Francis."

"I hope it's Francis," my wife said.

We went through the possibilities.

"Your stories are all about how we have no money. Some reader of *Vogue* or *Harper's* after reading one decided —"

"The fishmonger," I interrupted, "probably forgot to put the card in. Good night."

But it bothered us.

We had the O'Caseys in, Doreen and Breon, for a smoked salmon treat. They also had young children and money was tight. I did large slices cut thin with more lemon and brown bread and pepper. They said it was delicious and nothing like that had ever happened to them.

Then on December 22 the cheque came from *Harper's Bazaar*. And I felt like a new person. I gave my wife most of the money — paid the milkman and part of the bill we owed at the Co-op. We got the last tree from the greengrocer. And the children and my wife suddenly got into the swing of things. I went out and got some greenery to put up around the rooms near the ceiling. They put up decorations . . . small presents began to appear under the tree . . . neatly wrapped up. The schoolkids, when they knocked on the front door after singing a carol, now got a few pennies. And later, at night, in a light rain, there was the massed choir in the street, men and women dressed all in black singing *While Shepherds Watched Their Flocks by Night* unaccompanied. They held flashlights under their chins and umbrellas above them . . . beautiful sound . . . their voices clear. Then they walked up the slope, in the dark, regrouped . . . and sang some more . . . the flashlights lighting up their faces.

Next day there was a letter from Canada, from my mother, with a twenty-five pound money order for the children. And in the evening Morley and Florrie came. (He was a farmer near Truro and ran a butcher shop and she had the postal substation — my wife was evacuated there during the war.) They came with their day's takings in a carrier bag and gave us a goose and a chicken. I cut some of the smoked salmon while my wife told them what happened.

"Well, I never —" Florrie said.

"It's very good," Morley said.

Next morning before seven I was at St Erth station waiting for the train to come. I was there to meet my wife's mother who had recently become a widow and was coming on the overnight train from London. I walked up and down the open platform to try and keep warm. Over to the west the clouds were low and grey. And one cloud, like a smudge, detached itself and was moving closer. I watched it. Suddenly I realized it wasn't a cloud but starlings. They came just over my head — and above and below, on either side of the tracks. Thousands of them. It felt as if I was in a black snowstorm. And the continual sound of their wings.

Then just as suddenly it went quiet. The train arrived, no one got out. A porter ran up to me. "Are you waiting for a lady?"

"Yes."

"I can't wake her up."

It was my mother-in-law having difficulty keeping her eyes open. I put on her sheepskin jacket, took her case, and the porter and I got her into a taxi. Her chin was on her chest.

I managed to wake her up on the drive back.

"What happened?"

"I took some drink on the train — to help me sleep — then a sleeping pill —"

"How many pills did you take?"

"One — two —"

Her head went down again.

When I got her into the house I told my wife what happened and to make a large jug of coffee. We forced her to drink. Then held her up, one on each side, and began to walk up and down the room and in the hallway, her feet dragging, I slapped her face when she closed her eyes, gave her more coffee, and continued walking. We did that for over an hour until she could stand by herself.

"I'm all right now," she said. She looked worn out. "I'll go upstairs and lie down and have a rest." She slept right through until next morning.

In the morning I made a fire in the front room. The pile of presents under the tree had grown almost overnight. Then, when we were all down, we sat on chairs, the children on the floor. My wife brought in a pot of hot coffee. And after we had coffee I started to give out the presents. One for each, and I would wait until the person opened it. Then I'd go to the next. The children saved their wrapping paper . . . the pile of presents by them.

And later we went into the next room and sat around the large dining-room table, dressed in the new sweater, the new shirt. A fire was going in the fireplace. The kids' paper chains were crisscrossing from the ceiling. And I had tacked some branches of ivy on the top of the walls as well.

We began with the last of the smoked salmon. Then the goose was brought in . . . and the vegetables . . . I poured brandy on the pudding and lit it. . . . And it burned with a blue flame.

We had finished the pudding and sat around the table with paper hats on our heads, when Martha had to go upstairs. When she came back she said, "Dad, there's a goat on the front steps by the door nibbling at the tree."

We went to the front room, to the window. And there was a dirty billy goat with part of an old torn rope hanging from its neck dragging on the ground. It was on the front granite steps nibbling at the pittosporum.

And we all laughed. It was so dirty and bedraggled and it didn't look domestic at all. It was black with some hairs that might have been white but were now dirty grey. The hairs were matted together and of different lengths. When it went down the slope, to the next house, I opened the front door and we went out. And watched it go, slowly, down the street. Stopping at the front gardens, the front steps, or staying on the sidewalk, then standing in the middle of the road. It looked so out of place in this suburban street of terraced houses.

Then I saw that the whole street was now out ... in small groups ... in front of their doors ... or on their steps. Some, like us, with paper hats still on their heads. And everyone was laughing or smiling and talking ... and looking at the goat.

Someone must have called the police. For later I heard they brought the goat back to the farmer, a few miles from here, who reported it missing.

On December 28, I couldn't put it off any longer. I wrote to the fishmonger whose address was on the label. Two and a half weeks later a letter arrived. In large, almost childish, writing it said:

Dublin, 4 January

Dear Sir,
I am pleased you enjoyed the salmon. We received a money order for same with instructions to send to you. It was signed, "anonymous gift."
Yours truly
P.J. Nolan

A MARITIME STORY

A MARITIME STORY

When I think of Max Bleenden I see him driving a long red car in Fredericton, dressed in grey flannels, a navy blue blazer or (if it was warm) a light purple shirt, and smoking a Gauloise. He looks solid. Broad shoulders, a strong neck, a wide face. His dark wavy hair is brushed back and receding. There is a slightly crooked smile. He wears glasses. The eyes are brown. In public he has the air of a celebrity. People look pleased when they say, "Hello, Dr Bleenden." I can hear him come up the worn steps of the George hotel, knock on the grey-painted door of my rented rooms. When I open the door he speaks in a rough low voice that has something of Europe in it.

"Can you lend me five dollars? I forgot to go to the bank. I have the gardener coming this morning. And I need to buy some tea and eggs. It's a tradition. I always make breakfast for the gardener."

I would give him the money then make some coffee while he looked around at the way I was living in this hotel with the second-hand furniture, the worn linoleum.

"I envy you," he said. "You live such a simple life. Mine is complicated."

Later, leaving Fredericton, he was driving me to the airport. We were silent. Suddenly he said, "You're going away . . . that's awful . . . I won't have anyone to talk to. There's no one down here."

I came to the Maritimes in 1965 because of Max Bleenden.

He had written to me in England. He said he liked my short stories. Would I like to come to Fredericton and be resident writer. And because we needed the money I said yes. I owed rent for two years. Had a lawyer's letter threatening action from the landlady's son. The landlady was a nice old lady who apologized for this. It only came out when she was sick. Her son happened to see what I owed.

I left wife and children behind — I had no intention of settling in the Maritimes — and flew over at the end of August.

Max Bleenden was to meet me in the lobby of the Beaverbrook Hotel. As he came in he looked around expectantly. But as soon as he saw me he looked disappointed.

"I didn't think you would be so short."

Max was several inches shorter. He drove me to his house — a solid greystone facing the river with a gravel drive, grass on either side, and a heavy front wooden door. Behind the house were tall trees and large gardens of fruit, vegetables, and flowers. Inside, the rooms were high, painted white, and lightly furnished with antique wooden furniture and blue carpets. On the walls were abstract oil paintings, and a photograph of a serious young girl. There were irises, roses, gladioli, in different colours, in glass vases and earthenware pots. There was a glass bowl full of fruit.

His wife came in. She was a bit taller than Max. Thin and shy with red hair. When she smiled she looked like a pretty Tallulah Bankhead. She hardly spoke. If I spoke to her, she smiled back. We sat in the comfortable chairs, in one of the front rooms, looking out at the river, and had tea.

A large elderly woman in grey walked in with sandwiches on a tray. As she went out Max said:

"She is here to look after my mother. My mother's name is Nettie. I want you to meet her."

He led me up the stairs, past three rooms, to a bare white room where a small elderly woman sat in a highbacked chair. Her hands were clutching the arm-rests. Her feet were not touching the ground. She was dressed in a purple blouse, a black skirt. Around her neck a light silk lemon scarf was tied loosely. Her grey hair was cut short and permed and I could see the pink scalp between curls. She sat by a window and beside a fish tank that had three small fish swimming in it. Max introduced me.

"Who are you?" his mother said in a flat voice.

"I'm Max's friend."

"Do you live here?"

"Yes."

She looked out of the window at the road, the river, the far shore, the sky.

"I write to Max every week," she said. "Did you know I'm going to Canada?"

She left us again. Went back to the window.

She had an interesting but worn-out face. She must have been pretty for the structure was still there with the prominent cheekbones, the small mouth with the noticeable front teeth as if a smile was never far away.

"I hate this house," she said. "It goes quiet. I don't know where everyone is."

She looked at the tank.

"They are trying to fob me off with fish. I don't want fish. I want people."

She looked at me.

"Suddenly it's quiet," she said. "They don't explain things. I don't know where they are. I don't know when they are coming back. They don't ask me if I want to go. They just go away. . . .

"Did you know I'm going to Canada? To the Maritimes. I have a son in the Maritimes."

Max began to walk impatiently up and down. She followed his movements. When he stopped near her she said:

"How long am I going to stay here?"

"How long would you like to stay, mother?" Max said. "For ever?"

"That's not very long," she said.

As I was leaving, Max said he and his wife were driving to Boston tomorrow for a short holiday before the academic year started. Would I like to come?

When we got to Boston all Max wanted to see were films. We saw six films in three days. He also wanted to go to a striptease. We went into a dark place where a young girl with long legs performed on a small stage, in the centre of the room, while the customers stood around and watched. A cigarette girl, not young, came by. Max picked up a small cigar, from her tray, and took out a coin from his pocket.

"Can I put a quarter in your box?" he asked with a grin.

"Don't be an asshole," the cigarette girl said. "You can't get into my box for a quarter."

She couldn't have known that she was talking to the Dean of a university.

On the drive back from Boston, with his wife asleep, Max told me about himself. He was born in Hamburg. "Both my parents spoke Yiddish. I also spoke Yiddish. But I have long forgotten it." His father was a publisher. They had a comfortable life. When he was thirteen — it was 1933 — his mother brought him to London. They didn't see his father again. He went to an English grammar school, then London University. They had little money. His mother did a variety of jobs, whatever she could get. It was while he was at university that his poems began to appear in the little magazines. His reviews in the weeklies. And talks on the BBC. That's when I first heard of him. But we never met. Although I used to go to the same Soho clubs, the same pubs: the French, Joe Lyons, the Mandrake.

Max said he played the piano, for a while, at the Colony. And we talked about Muriel Belcher and Francis Bacon. After the war ("My father was a conscientious objector . . . his father was a conscientious objector . . . so I was a conscientious objector. I was sent to work on the land. I was digging ditches. And all I wanted to do was fly a Spitfire") he came to Canada to lecture at a small college in Nova Scotia where he met his wife, the daughter of a General. She inherited money. They moved to Fredericton. "After I married, the writing stopped. The instinct for it had gone. And I haven't written anything since. But I can tell the real thing when I see it. And *boychick*," he slapped my knee, "you have it."

But despite this friendliness I was uncomfortable with Max.

In the first week of term he asked me to meet his creative writing class. There were about twenty students, mostly girls. "Here is our resident writer," Max began. "He writes short stories. They are mostly stories about being hard-up. But look the way he is dressed. He is wearing an expensive English suit, expensive English shoes, an expensive shirt and tie."

I didn't know where to look.

(The thin light-grey suit I bought in a discount house in Truro, Cornwall, for nine pounds. It was made in Bulgaria. My shoes, also cheap, I bought in Exeter. They were made in Romania.)

I also disliked the way he took it for granted that I would just fall in with his plans. He never asked.

He just said, "Let's go —," or, "I'll pick you up for a football game at —."

My reaction to this was immediate.

When I was supposed to be at the President's reception to introduce new members I was in the Riverside Room of the Beaverbrook Hotel drinking a beer and reading a thriller.

Next morning he came to my office, three doors away from his. A hurt expression on his face.

"Why weren't you at the President's reception?"

"When was it?"

"Yesterday. I made a speech telling all about you. People clapped. We waited for you to step forward. Nothing happened."

I turned down all invitations.

Max would walk briskly into my office and say: "I just had a phone call from the Rotarians. They have a monthly meeting. The food is very good. They would like you to be their next speaker —"

"I'm busy," I said. "Working."

I wasn't working. I was moving. From the Beaverbrook, that he put me in, to the George, which was less than half the price. I was also getting to know Fredericton. The long residential streets with the front lawns and the large wooden houses with verandahs and trees. The short business streets, by the river, with the small stores and Chinese restaurants. But it didn't take long to walk through it. And I had a feeling of isolation, of being cut off.

One morning I walked to the supermarket by the river to get some groceries. When I came out a mild man in glasses, dressed like a farmer, came up to me.

"Have you got education?"

I didn't know what to say.

"Have you got education?"

I thought this was a new way of asking for money.

"Yes," I said hesitantly.

"What is eight at fifty dollars each?"

"Four hundred dollars."

"Four hundred," he said loudly. And repeated it as if he didn't believe it. He walked away delighted.

Another day I went to the Legislative building. I was listening to a debate on fishing from the public gallery when an usher came up to me and whispered:

"Sir, you can't sit like that."

I had my legs crossed.

"Why not?"

"The members below — they can see."

"I'm wearing trousers."

"It's a rule sir . . . because of the ladies. They'd come here . . . sit like you . . . and from below, with some, you could see the time of day."

On Armistice Day I went to the cenotaph. A service of remembrance was going on. Names of local people killed in the Second World War were being read over a loudspeaker. The voice said:

Graham Budd, Royal Canadian Air Force.

Robert Pichette, Royal Canadian Corps of
Signals.
Jim Smith, Royal Canadian Air Force.

Brought to you by Frank's Fast Foods. . . .

Tommy Symons, Royal Canadian Navy.
Fred Towers, Royal Canadian Engineers.

Brought to you by Dominion Supermarket. . . .

I wasn't sleeping well. At first light I'd walk to
the river to see the trees in their autumn colours,
the solitary white house on the far shore, reflected
in the water. After breakfast, I'd go out again, buy a
paper. Then to the post office to see if there were
any letters from my wife. I wrote three times,
sometimes more, a week (as she did) telling her I
missed her. That I disliked being here. And
couldn't wait to get back. Meanwhile I was going
to earn as much money as I could.
    With this in mind I walked to the newspaper
building in the Square. And was shown into the
owner's empty office. The owner walked in. Small
stubby brown shoes with thick heels and thick
soles and rounded tops. A black eye-patch over his
right eye. He was about five foot ten. He had a
small moustache, thin dark hair, and spoke in a
clipped English voice. He was referred to as the
Brigadier. And told me he was a friend of Beaverbrook, knew the Duke and Duchess of Windsor
and, for my benefit, he talked about Arnold Bennett. He said that when Arnold Bennett reviewed a

book in the *Evening Standard* the book would sell out. He would give me a page, in his monthly magazine for the Maritimes, and he expected me to do the same as Arnold Bennett.

But the books I wanted were published in London. And often they didn't want to send review copies to a Maritime monthly they hadn't heard of. The Brigadier was furious. I saw him pick up the phone, in a rage, and shout to the London publisher demanding a copy. Sometimes it worked.

I did articles on an anthology of short stories, a novel by Graham Greene, books on Hemingway, Babel, Chekhov, and an anthology of the Second World War. I also had some of my stories reprinted. From this I earned an extra five hundred dollars a month.

It was by doing this work that I met the journalists who worked for the Brigadier. They were young Englishmen, from English public schools, that the Brigadier brought over. Their calling cards said *Gentlemen of the Farm*. They lived in a run-down rented farm across the river. In the city they wore suits, ties, clean shirts. I expected a rolled umbrella, a bowler hat. And when they played cricket or soccer, against the university or the Army Camp, their sports clothes were immaculate. But on the farm — they only had chickens — they wore worn-out shabby clothes. They went around unshaven, uncombed. The rooms had disorder and chicken shit. The kitchen looked as if no one had washed-up for months or put the garbage out. . . .

When I went for my early evening drink to the Beaverbrook, I would join these neatly dressed journalists and listen as they joked, discussed life and the world situation.

With them, sometimes, was Marcel, a French Canadian from Moncton. He was in computers. He drove a green MG. He was convinced that I was getting the wrong impression of the Maritimes by mixing too much with intellectuals and people with money. So he took me to various beer parlours. Then, to the outskirts, off the highway, and on to a dirt road, to a string of unpainted wooden shacks spaced far apart. Smoke came from a tin chimney. No one was outside.

Marcel then drove to an Indian reservation. The same signs of poverty and hopelessness. As if everyone inside was lying fully-dressed on a bed, not sleeping, in the middle of the afternoon.

"I don't read books," Marcel said on the drive back, "but I'll read one of yours. If I like it — I'll buy it."

Max came to the George.

"Have you been avoiding me? It's over two weeks since I've seen you."

"I haven't," I said.

"Come for a ride."

Then he said: "Let's go back to my place for a drink. I'm depressed."

When we got out of the car instead of going into the house he went around it. We cast long shadows on the grass. He led me to the trees. And, among them, to a wooden hut. He unlocked the door.

Inside it was spartan. A plain wooden table. An ordinary wooden chair. Used books on planks of wood held up by bricks. An open fireplace with sawn wood stacked beside it. There were picture-postcards stuck on the walls of paintings by Rembrandt, Monet, Pissarro, Chagall, Bonnard. A small sink, a single tap, an electric kettle. Empty jars of instant coffee, packs of Gauloises and matches. A bottle of Rémy Martin was by a small radio. A used upright piano by a wall. Beside another, a couch was made up as a bed.

"I feel at home here," Max said. "The house . . . that's my wife's place. This is mine." He indicated the books, the faded poster of *The Threepenny Opera* on a wall, the faded magazines.

I looked at the books. I knew them. They were English books of the late 1940s and 1950s. He showed me magazines with his poems, his reviews.

"That was my time," Max said. "Who knows what I would have done had I stayed in Europe. But I'm here. And, *boychick*, most of the time I like it."

He showed me letters he had from T.S. Eliot, Picasso. And, from another folder, he brought out obituaries that he had cut from *The Times*. They were of writers, painters, editors of little magazines, who were known just after the war and who died young. They were people I also knew.

"That's why we get on," Max said. "We have the same references."

The only sign of luxury was a large window looking out to the trees and gardens. "I come here when I can," Max said. "In the morning the dew is on the grass . . . the birds have started . . . the flowers are at their best . . . I read, I smoke, I have a drink. I listen to the BBC overseas service for the news . . . I play the piano . . . I day-dream. It's my bolt-hole. Then I go to work."

He poured Rémy Martin into the cracked cups. He sat on the couch. I, on the wooden chair. He lit up a Gauloise.

"I read the same books again and again," Max said. "Now that I don't write — I copy out things that I like." He opened a thick notebook, turned some pages, and read aloud.

" 'The heart — it's worth less than people think. It's quite accommodating, it accepts anything. It's not particular. But the body — that's different — it has a cultivated taste — it knows what it wants.'

"You know who said that?"

"No."

"Colette." He turned more pages. Read out: "to exist is enough." Then turned to the last page of the notebook, showed it to me. The only thing on it was: "The final unimportance of human life."

"Who said that?"

"I don't know," Max said. "I didn't. But when I read it — I don't feel so bad."

He put out a Gauloise, lit another.

"I'll miss Fredericton —"

"When are you leaving?"

"When I'm 65, I'll retire to England. Somewhere in the country. Not too far from London."

"And your wife?"

"She won't want to come. But when the time comes she'll go. As you see, my wife and I don't talk much. Not now. We keep certain thoughts to ourselves."

We finished the brandy in the cups. He locked the door. We were walking to the house when his wife came quickly towards us.

"Nettie's escaped."

"When?"

"I don't know. I went into her room. And she wasn't there."

"I'll use the car," Max said. "You," he said to his wife, "look in the restaurants, the library, the stores."

"I'll look for her," I said.

"Fine. Do the side streets and by the river."

"What was she wearing?"

"A pink sweater," his wife said, "grey skirt and slippers."

I walked and looked for over an hour and a half. No sign of Nettie. I phoned up Max, from a call-box, wondering if she was still alive.

"The police have her," he said calmly. "I'm going just now to the station to pick her up. She was trying to get on a bus. She had no money. She told them she was going to Canada."

"Has this happened before?"

"Yes," he said.

Two weeks later it was a different Max who came to the George. He had come back from a three-day conference in Calgary. And he talked non-stop

about women. "It's all in the angle of penetra-
tion. . . . If they have large bums . . . it's better to use
a pillow. I picked up a professor at the hotel bar
about thirty-five or thirty-six . . . a medievalist. . . . I
asked her to spend the night with me. She said she
would if I promised I wouldn't do anything."

"What happened?"

He looked surprised. "Nothing happened. I
gave her my word."

That night he picked me up for the annual party
of his creative writing class. The parents, he said,
were away. "We'll enjoy ourselves." There were
drinks, music, food. Max was the first one to start
dancing. Then spent the rest of the evening, in a
dark corner, with the girl who was giving the
party. When he drove me back to the George he
was like an adolescent. "Now you see why I have
these creative writing classes."

"Better wipe the lipstick off before you go in the
house."

Next morning he walked into my office. He was
excited.

"I needed a new secretary," he said. "They sent
me one. But I'll have to let her go. I couldn't work
with her."

"Why not?"

"Too sexy. Come, I'll show you."

He led me down the corridor to the main office.
And introduced me to this young tall girl who was
smiling. She looked like girls I saw in the street.
Blonde short hair, healthy, outdoor type, in a tight
sweater and a tight skirt.

"Turn around," Max said.

And she did, as if she were a fashion model, still smiling.

"How could I work standing close to her?"

"She probably needs the job," I said.

"She'll go back to the typing pool. Alone with her . . . I wouldn't trust myself."

I liked Max better when the macho side of him was absent. One afternoon he picked me up and drove by the river into the country for about an hour. "I make this trip about once every six or seven weeks," he said. "My wife goes more often. We have a daughter. She lives by herself, a solitary. She's a lovely girl, twenty-four, you'll see."

We went down a dirt track. There was a wooden shack with asbestos on the outside and on the roof. In a clearing, a small vegetable garden and some flowers. A brown dog came out and a black and ginger kitten. The dog barked. A voice said,

"What is it, Fred?"

Then Max's daughter came out of the shack. She was tall and slim and she looked like one of those Pre-Raphaelite paintings. She ran over and kissed Max.

"Hello, Dad."

He introduced me. She looked a bit shy. She spoke softly. She brought us inside . . . made some coffee.

There were different herbs . . . books to do with the psyche . . . Buddhism . . . happiness . . . there were plants growing in small pots . . . lots of paperback books . . . and postcards put up. . . .

I went out to leave them alone.

We stayed about an hour.

Max didn't talk much on the drive back. "Every time I come back from seeing her I feel sad. And there is nothing I can do."

Before driving to the airport, I went with Max to see Nettie in her room. I told her I was leaving. But she took no notice. Max had bought her a colour television for her seventieth birthday. She was watching a train going across the country from the Atlantic to the Pacific. It was a travelogue showing the different provinces in the autumn.

When it was over Nettie was silent.

Then she said to Max:

"Why did you keep that country all to yourself?"

I returned to England, to my wife and kids, paid off the debts. Had a three-week holiday with the family in London. And there was enough money left for the next nine months. I began to write.

All the time I was in Fredericton, I thought I hated it. But bits and pieces began to appear in my next novel and in several short stories.

Max and I wrote regularly. He always included small details that I suspect he thought I might be able to use.

> "... on a freezing night our mayor was pushed out of a moving car on the main street at three in the morning. He was pushed out by a lady who wasn't his wife. He was in the nude.... They tried to burn the George down twice since you left ... both times the fire engines arrived too soon.... The Brigadier died while on holiday in the Bahamas.... The Gentlemen of the Farm

gave a farewell party . . . they are leaving for British Columbia. Sometime after midnight we went out of the farmhouse and there was a large wooden cross burning fiercely. Someone said: Ku Klux Klan. Someone else said: This is New Brunswick. . . ."

At Christmas he sent five pounds to each of our daughters.

The following summer he and his wife came to see us. They were travelling through the South-West in a rented car. In St Ives they stayed in the best hotel, the Tregenna Castle. Max took us there for a meal. As we entered, and saw the glass chandeliers, he said,

"Ribbentrop was promised this hotel for his residence by Hitler after he conquered England."

Next day it rained. They stayed with us in the house. Max played ping-pong with the children. Then records. *Hair* was in fashion. Max played it over and over. He twisted to the music, he sang the songs, he liked the naughty words ("Mummy, Mummy, what is fellatio?"). He tried to get my wife to dance on the table.

That is how I remembered him on that cool September morning when I heard that he and his wife were killed when their car went off the highway.

Later that day I wrote his obituary for *The Times*.

I came again to Fredericton, eighteen years later, this summer, to give a lecture. I stayed at the Beaverbrook. After a good breakfast, by a window facing the river, I went for a walk. I walked along the main street and to the side street where the George was. It was burned out ... gutted. Planks of charred wood were hanging precariously. And where I had my rooms I could see blue sky.

Wherever I walked I kept remembering Max. And things that happened. But for some reason I couldn't find my way to the university. I asked a woman on the opposite side of the street. She said she was going part of the way. She told me she came from Ontario, from Hamilton. And couldn't wait to get back. They had another year here — until their only daughter finished school.

"This is failure city," she said.

I walked up the slope, by the trees and the grass of the university. They named a new building after him — Max Bleenden Hall — a girls' residence. And on the quarter-hour the clock, above its entrance, has a delicate chime.

DJANGO, KARFUNKELSTEIN, & ROSES

DJANGO, KARFUNKELSTEIN, & ROSES

In late October, on the morning of my fiftieth birthday, we had breakfast early — my wife and three daughters. On the plain wooden table: a black comb, a half-bottle of brandy, a red box of matches from Belgium, a felt pen, a couple of Dutch cigars, a card of Pissarro's "Lower Norwood under Snow," and a record. They wished me Happy Birthday. And we kissed.

After breakfast the children went to school. We continued to talk, without having to finish sentences, over another cup of coffee. Then my wife went to make the beds, water the plants, do the washing. And I went to the front room, lit the coal fire, smoked a Dutch cigar, drank some of the brandy, put the record on, listened to Django Reinhardt and Stephane Grappelli — The Hot Club of France. And looked out for the postman.

The mimosa tree was still in bloom in the small front garden as were some roses. To the left, a road

95

of terraced houses curved as it sloped down to the church steeple and the small shops. And at the end of the road — above houses, steeple, shops — was the white-blue of the bay.

Directly opposite, past the garden and across the road, was Wesley Street. A short narrow street of stone cottages. I watched the milkman leave bottles on the granite by the front doors. Mr Veal — a tall man with glasses, a retired carpenter, a Plymouth brethren ("I have my place up there when I die," he told me pointing to the sky) — came out of his cottage holding a white tablecloth. He shook the tablecloth in the street. From the slate roofs, the red chimney pots, came jackdaws, sparrows, and a few gulls. They were waiting for him. Mr Veal swirled the tablecloth — as if it was a cape — and over his shoulder it folded neatly on his back. He stood in the centre of the street with the white tablecloth on his back, the birds near his feet. ("I need to get wax out of my ears," he said when we were walking. "I don't hear people — but I hear the birds.") Then he went inside.

The postman appeared and walked past the house. This morning it didn't matter. My wife hung the washing in the courtyard and pulled up the line. Then left the house to buy the food for the day. The sun came through the coloured glass of the inside front door and onto the floor in shafts of soft yellow, blue, and red. I went upstairs to the large attic room. And got on with the new story . . .

Within a few years this life changed. And for my wife it ended. The children left home. I would get up early — the gulls woke me — wondering what to do. (I wasn't writing anything.) Living by one-self like this, I thought, how long the day is. How slow it goes by. I went from one empty room to another . . . looked outside . . . such a nice looking place . . . and wondered how to go on. And there were times when I wondered why go on?

Then a letter came from Zurich. It came from the people who worked in a literary agency. They told me that my literary agent was going to be seventy. They were planning a surprise party. Could I come?

At the airport a young man with curly brown hair and glasses, just over medium height, was holding a sheet of paper with my name on it. He was shy. (No, he hadn't been waiting long.) He smiled easily. He said he did the accounts.

"You have not met Ruth?"

"No," I said.

"How long is she your agent?"

"Fourteen years."

Zurich was busy. In sunny end-of-May weather he drove to the heights above . . . to a cul-de-sac of large houses. They had signs, *Achtung Hund* . . . except in front of the large house where he stopped.

As he opened the door there were red roses, in the hallway, lots of them. And more red roses at the bottom of the wide stairs. The wall opposite the front door was mostly books. But in a space, waist high, a small sink with the head of a brass lion. Water came out of its mouth. There were more roses, as well as books, in the large carpeted rooms that he led me through. Then outside, down a few steps, to a grass lawn. People were standing in clusters talking and eating. A tall attractive woman with straight blonde hair was cooking over a barbecue. She talked loudly in Italian. A man in his thirties — regular clean-cut face, black curly hair — was moving around slowly with a hand-held camera, stopping, then moving again.

The person at the airport came towards me with a lively short woman. She looked very alert, intelligent, and with a sense of fun.

"What a surprise," she said. We embraced quickly and kissed. Then we moved apart and looked at one another.

"This is very moving," she said quietly.

I could hear the whirr of the film camera.

"You must be hungry."

She linked arms, led me to the barbecue, and introduced me to Giuli — the tall blonde Italian who was her housekeeper. (She would die, unexpectedly, in two years.) There were frankfurters, hamburgers, salad, grapes. I had a couple of frankfurters and walked to the lawn's edge and to an immediate drop. The churches, the buildings, the houses of Zurich spread out below and in front. Across some water I could see wooded hills. And further away, hardly visible against the skyline, mountains.

More people kept arriving. I could now hear French and German. It was pleasantly warm. Sparrows flitted around us. Giuli, and others, threw them bits of bread.

That night cars brought the guests into Zurich. The birthday party was in a Guildhall near the centre. A narrow river was outside. The water looked black. I could see several white swans on it. The guests came from different parts of Western Europe. They were mostly publishers. But I did meet Alfred Andersch. A gentle man with a pleasant face, a nice smile ("Why write novels if you can write short stories"). He would die within a year. And Elias Canetti. A short stocky man with a large face, high forehead, thick black hair brushed back. (He would be awarded the Nobel Prize.)

There were speeches, toasts, in English. Then the guests went in line to another room where — on a long table with white tablecloths — there were lit candles and all sorts of food. Platters of shrimps . . . asparagus . . . a large cooked salmon . . . roast beef . . . the salads were colourful. I looked ahead to the far end where the cakes were. And saw, on the table, what I thought was one of the white swans from the river. As I came closer I realized it was made of butter.

Later that night, in the house, seven of us who were staying as guests sat with Ruth in the kitchen. We talked and drank. I was the only male. The women's ages spread from the late thirties into the seventies. The youngest was the girl from upstairs who rented a room and worked in Zurich. She was waiting for her gentleman friend to phone to let her know when he would be in Zurich. After she spoke to him she came down and joined us. She started to sing, *It's All Right With Me*. She had a fine voice. We joined in. There were more Cole Porter songs. And Jerome Kern. Then the older ladies sang, very enthusiastically, European Socialist songs. And went on to folk songs, mostly German. (Ruth was born in Hamburg.) The one that made an impression was a slow sad tune about The Black Death.

Giuli, sitting beside me, said in broken English how her husband, a pilot in the Italian air force, was killed while flying. And how lucky she was to find Ruth. Then, with more wine, she began to talk Italian to everyone and stood up wanting us all to dance. We formed a chorus line, Ruth in the middle. We kicked our legs and sang as we moved around the kitchen. Then tired we sat down. This time Ruth was beside me, a little out of breath. While our glasses were being filled again I asked her — what was she thinking when she saw those large bunches of roses all over the house?

And she said that during the last war she worked as a courier for the Resistance. They sent her to Holland. The Nazis tracked her down. "Things became difficult. I was on a wanted list. I had to stay inside my small room. I couldn't go out.

"In the next room there was a man called Karfunkelstein. He told me he was going to commit suicide. I asked him why.

'One can't live with a name like Karfunkelstein in these times.'

"I managed to talk him out of it.

" 'Wait,' he said. And left me.

"When he came back he had his arms full of roses and other flowers.

" 'For you,' he said.

And gave them to me.

"My small room was full of flowers. And I couldn't go out to sell a rose for food."

Four and a half years later, early this December, I saw Ruth again. I had been invited to Strasbourg to give a lecture at the university. After the lecture I took a train to Zurich. Outside the station I went into a waiting taxi. I gave the driver the name of the street.

He replied with the number I wanted.

"How did you know?"

"Many people go there."

This time no guests or flowers. But the same warm welcome. The young man who met me at the airport was still doing the accounts, still looked shy, and smiled easily. His hair was grey. I met the new housekeeper, Juliette. She came from France. About the same age as Ruth.

It was cold and foggy. At dusk I could see the lights of Zurich below. Juliette brought in some coffee and for over an hour Ruth and I talked business. She phoned up the Canadian Embassy in Bonn and spoke to the cultural attaché about an East German translation. She phoned a radio station in Cologne about a short story that had been broadcast. We went over a contract line by line. Then Ruth said,

"I must go and lie down for twenty minutes."

She went upstairs. I went into the kitchen. And talked to Juliette while she was preparing the food. Juliette told me she used to be a photographer in Paris before the war. Then worked in London. She had a studio in Knightsbridge. And talked nostalgically of the time she lived there. A small radio was on. Someone was playing a guitar. I said I liked Django Reinhardt.

"I knew him," Juliette said. "My husband André was his best friend for some years."

Ruth appeared looking less tired.

"You didn't stay twenty minutes," Juliette said in mock anger.

Ruth and I finished the rest of our business over a drink. Then it was time for supper. The three of us sat around a small table in the kitchen, in a corner, by the stove. We had red wine. We clinked glasses and drank to our next meeting.

Juliette passed the salad bowl.

I asked her about Django Reinhardt.

"He couldn't read or write. He was a gypsy," she said. "Very black hair but good white teeth. You know how he got those two fingers? His wife was in a caravan making artificial flowers when there was a fire. Django ran in and saved her. His hand was burned. . . . Oh, he was a bad driver. He had so many accidents . . . the car looked a wreck. One time he came to see us with a new shirt, a tie, and a new suit. He asked my husband what was the proper way to wear it? André showed him. Django stood in front of the mirror wearing the new clothes, looking at himself, very pleased at the way he looked." (Juliette acted this out with little movements of her face and hands as she spoke.) "We listened to him play . . . he would play for hours . . . if I could have recorded it. . . . He only began to make records so he could give them to his friends.

But he could be difficult. To get him to the record-ing studio on time my husband would say: 'Django, you are late . . . the machinery is all set up . . . there are people waiting . . . they have their jobs.' And Django would not go. André tried again. And Django got angry.

" 'I need my freedom. If I can't have my freedom . . . it's not my life.'

"Later he bought a château near Paris. That life didn't suit him. He was ruined . . . by money . . . by women . . . fame. He couldn't handle it."

Juliette stood up and from the stove, brought a small casserole and served the meat and the vege-tables.

"What happened to Karfunkelstein?" I asked Ruth.

"He probably committed suicide," she said in a flat voice. "In those days people like him did . . .

"On May 10th 1940," she went on, "the Germans came into Holland. Next day there was an epi-demic of suicides. There weren't enough coffins. They put them in sacks.

"I knew this young family. They had two small boys. The man was a teacher. His wife was in love with him. She would go along with whatever he wanted. And he wanted to commit suicide. He kept saying: 'Life as it is going to be . . . will not be worth living.'

"I knew someone in the American Embassy. I arranged for them to see him next morning so they could get out of Holland. But I wanted to make sure they would be there.

"I went to their house. The man was still saying that life without freedom to live the way he had lived would be impossible . . . when the youngest boy swallowed a small bulb from a flashlight. (At least his mother said that he did.) She was very worried. She asked me: What should she do? How could she get a doctor? After a while the child got better. Because I saw how worried she had been I thought it was all right to leave them for the night. I said I would be back in the morning.

"When I arrived, the two boys were dead. The man and the wife had sealed all the doors and windows. Turned on the gas. And they had cut their wrists."

When we had finished, Juliette began to clear and wash up while Ruth went into the other room to dictate letters into a machine for the secretary next morning. I went up to the room where I would sleep the night — a large bare room in the attic with a low double bed, books all over, and a wide window with a view of Zurich. I looked at the lights and thought of the people who had come to Zurich, from other countries, for different reasons. And how few of them stayed.

Juliette came to the door and said, "There is a Canadian film on television. Have you heard of it? It is called *Mon Oncle Antoine*."

"It's the best Canadian film I have seen," I said.

"Then we shall all see it," she said.

I went down with her.

Juliette drew the curtains. Ruth put in a hearing aid. "I only do this for television," she said.

I looked forward to seeing the film again. I had seen it, about twenty years ago, in St Ives on television and remembered how moved I had been by it.

"There is a marvellous shot," I said while the news was on. "It is winter. On the extreme left of the picture there is a horse and a sleigh with a young boy and his uncle. The horse has stopped. And on the extreme right of the picture is a coffin that has fallen off the sleigh. In between there is this empty field of snow. It is night. The wind is blowing . . . no words are spoken. But that image I have remembered all these years."

Mon Oncle Antoine came on. The first surprise — it was in colour. I remembered it in black and white. Then I realized . . . it was because in St Ives we had then a black and white TV set. There were other disappointments. It might have been because of the German sub-titles, or my memory.

I told them the scene was about to come on.

When it did — it wasn't memorable at all.

Was it because it was in colour? Or had it been cut? I remembered it as lasting much longer. And it was the length of the shot, in black and white, that made it so poignant.

When the film was over I could see they were disappointed.

"I remember it differently," I said. And told them how I had seen it on a black and white TV set.

"It would have been better in black and white," Ruth said.

"There may have been cuts."

"It seemed very jumpy," Juliette said. "You could see it had the possibility of a good movie."

That night in the attic, in bed, I heard midnight by the different clocks in Zurich. I didn't count how many. But there were several. Each one starting a few seconds after another . . . and thought about *Mon Oncle Antoine*. How it differed from what I remembered. I saw how I had changed that shot. Just as I had switched the candles from around the man in the coffin at the start. And had them around the boy in the coffin at the end. I had, over the years, changed these things in order to remember them. Is this what time does? Perhaps it was a good film because it could suggest these things.

And was this what Juliette had done when she told about Django Reinhardt? And Ruth with Karfunkelstein?

But some things don't change.

I remembered my wife having to go into Penzance hospital to drain off some fluid. It was in the last two weeks of her life. She hadn't been outside for over a year but in that front room where I brought down a bed. And from there she looked out at the granite of Wesley Street and Mr Veal feeding the birds. Two men carried her out on a canvas and put her in the back of the ambulance.

When she returned she said, "It's so beautiful. The sky . . . the clouds . . . the trees . . . the fields . . . the hedges. I was lying on my back and I could see through the windows. . . ."

Early next morning Ruth drove me to the railway station. The streets were quite empty. The sun was not high above the horizon. And here it was snowing. The sun caught the glass of the buildings, the houses, and lit them up. And the snow was falling . . . thick flakes.

"My aunt in Israel is ninety," Ruth said. "And drives her car. Isn't that marvellous?"

We were going down a turning road, down a slope, then it straightened out. I asked her,

"Will you go on living in Zurich?"

"I don't know. The only other country would be Holland. I like Holland."

After she left I went inside the station and gave all the Swiss change I had to a plump young girl who was selling things from a portable kiosk. In return I had a bar of chocolate, a large green apple, and a yellow pack of five small cigars.

TRICKS

TRICKS

In the late spring, I received an invitation to tutor, for four days, a class of teachers in their final year of training. On a bright morning I set off for an estate in West Cornwall. I took the train to Penzance. Then a green country bus. It went slowly up a steep road. At the top it levelled out. We were on an open moor. It was exhilarating. I could see for miles. A brilliant blue sky. Haunches of earth with gorse and bracken and scattered granite boulders. The only sign that said people were about — a row of wooden telegraph poles, by the road, carrying a single wire.

I got off the bus, on a plateau, and walked with my bag along a rough dirt road. It brought me still higher onto the moor. A cool breeze. A smell of coconuts came from the gorse beside me. I watched three gulls fly over. They appeared to fly in slow motion. There were no sounds. Not a car, not a person.

When I saw the estate I didn't expect anything as isolated to be so grand. From the moor it was almost hidden by trees and a few granite boulders. And the boulders, made smooth by the centuries, were taller than the trees.

I swung open a heavy white gate and walked along a pebble drive. On either side — behind tall, trimmed green bushes — were thick sub-tropical gardens with flowers whose names I didn't know. Bright pinks, whites, orange, yellow, light and dark purples and blues. A gap . . . a low stone wall . . . and behind it a fruit garden. Another stone wall . . . and behind that a vegetable garden with a greenhouse.

The drive ended at the side of a large house with tall windows. A bus (*Hereford Education Authority* on its door) was parked by a used truck that had gardening tools. A path to the left of the house. Another to the right. I walked to the left, under a granite arch. And past the arch a sunken grass lawn neatly cut. The sunken grass lawn, with steep grass slopes, was sheltered on three sides by bushes, trees, and the front of the granite house. The wide other side was open. To the left — the upward sloping moor, and the road across it the bus had taken. While in front, and to the right, tall grass with campion and foxgloves. Then a sharp drop of bracken and gorse. Several hundred feet further down the bracken and the gorse levelled out to a patchwork of cultivated small green fields with hedgerows for fences and cows around an isolated farm. The small fields went right up to steep cliffs. And past the cliffs, to the horizon, was the sea.

Looking at all this, I didn't notice a tall man with a stick (who must have come from the house) walking towards me. His feet kicked out — slightly ahead and to the side — while he held his head and shoulders back, as if to balance his walk. It gave him a slightly arrogant presence, even when he smiled. Fine features in a longish heavy face, a strong jaw, thinning white hair combed back. He was neatly dressed in grey flannels, a light grey tweed jacket, a red-checked shirt, a dark blue tie. He looked English and vaguely familiar. He also looked out of place here. But so did the sunken lawn, the sub-tropical gardens, the large house.

"You a student?"

"No, a tutor."

"You must be the other one."

It was then that I recognized him. Eric Symes, a singer in musicals, looking much older than the photographs I had seen in newspapers and magazines. But they belonged to the time he was well known. When I used to hear him on the radio and on records.

"You will have the goosehouse," he indicated with his stick. "Past those trees. His is further along. After you leave your things go to the other side of the house to the kitchen. Meet your students. They arrived earlier. If there is anything you want — ask Connie."

We stood looking at the view, in silence, for several minutes.

"It's beautiful," I said.

"Yes," he said. "I have to fight to keep it this way. It's Bronze Age."

He began to walk . . . stiff and erect, using the stick, while his feet kicked out. I guess he had a stroke . . . along the top of the grass slope . . . by the sunken lawn . . . towards an opening. . . .

"Come and see me," he called back. "I'll show you the house and the gardens."

A half-hour later I was in a warm kitchen, by a scrubbed wooden table, having a coffee (a red enamel pot was kept warm on the Aga) looking, from a wide window, at the moor the sea the sky, and talking with some of the students.

When a taxi drove up. A tired-looking man, of average height, appeared. He wore a mustard, military cut overcoat and a black fedora. When he came in, carrying a green canvas bag, everyone stopped talking.

"I'm Adolphe Cayley," he said in a nervous voice.

He looked uncomfortable.

One of the girls said, "Like a coffee?"

"Thank you."

"Milk and sugar?"

"No. Black."

He had a few sips. Then walked over and asked if I was the other tutor. We shook hands formally. Coming closer he said. "Your first time, isn't it? Don't worry. I have done this many times. They usually send me to break someone in."

I had heard of Adolphe Cayley in much the same way as I had heard of Eric Symes. And in both cases

I met them too late. Adolphe Cayley was known because of a short poem he had written some forty years earlier. It was used in an understated English war film. I can't remember the lines. But it was how ordinary life, during a war, goes on. And will continue to go on after the war is over.

He took his glasses off. He had light grey eyes. And, with the other hand, rubbed them. He put the glasses back on and asked if I was Canadian. He said he had been in Canada as part of the Commonwealth Air Training Scheme.

"Did you fly?"

"No, I wrote propaganda."

He had a sister, he said, in Toronto that he visited.

I asked if he liked Toronto.

"It is very clean."

He kept wearing the black fedora. I thought he was bald. But later when he took it off his short straight hair was black, not a grey hair anywhere. And I knew he had to be in his sixties.

I also assumed he was English. But it was evident he was something else. When I finally asked him, he said, "I'm not thoroughbred. My mother is from France. When I'm introduced, if people look surprised, I tell them — like Hitler but with an e." He smiled. "Any of your books in print?"

Surprised by this directness I said "No."

"Neither are mine. So we both know why we are here."

The white shirt was frayed at the neck. There was a stain on his tie. His brown shoes had the leather split on top. And the heels were worn right

down. Yet despite his awkwardness and the out-
ward appearance the impression I had was of
someone with an inner dignity.

And the awkwardness also seemed to disappear
when he took charge. He told two students that
their jobs would be to go out every day and bring
back dead wood for the fireplace. He picked two
others, told them to see Connie in the office. She
would give them money and a list of food to buy in
Penzance for the rest of the week.

"We have to look after ourselves," he said.

On a sheet of paper he drew columns for the
days we would be here. And asked the students to
write their names for specific jobs.

"Every day two people will prepare lunch and
dinner. Two others will wash and clean up. At
breakfast we fend for ourselves. The best cooks will
be on the last night when the final meal will be
something special with wine."

That evening we had supper in the dining-room.
Bare timbers across the ceiling. A bright fire in the
large fireplace. We sat on fixed wooden benches by
wooden tables. While we were having coffee,
Adolphe stood up. "I thought," he said, "I would
say a few words before we begin.

"Tomorrow morning, at eight, we start to work.
I'll have seven — Peter will have seven. I'll pass
around these two pieces of paper. They are marked
for every half-hour of the morning with a five-
minute break. Put your name down for the time
you want to come. We will see you in that order.
We'll talk, give you assignments and, when you

write them, go over them. The rest of the time you are free to do what you like. There is a small library. There are rooms to be by yourself — though everything in them is faintly damp. There are good walks. This extraordinary landscape. And no distractions. No radio, no television, no newspapers. We are cut off —"

He drank some coffee.

"One of the things you need is a good pair of eyes. I was in Paris last summer. Walking in a street. When I saw, on the pavement, outside a shop, cages with small animals inside. In one cage were pigeons. They were pecking at the grain on the bottom of their cage . . . sending some of the grains outside. A lone pigeon came flying along the street. It landed beside the cage. It began to peck at the outside grains. Then at grains it could reach between the bars. Someone came from the shop, clapped her hands, 'Va-t-en.' The pigeon flew away. Those inside the cage went on pecking at the grain."

The students were making notes.

"Take things from life," Adolphe said. "Bad experience is better than no experience. Invent as little as possible. You are inventing the piece the way you use words and the way you are telling it. Wherever you go you will notice things.

"After Paris I went to a small provincial town. It was the end of July. All day Christmas carols were being played on loudspeakers in the streets. I got to know a teacher in this provincial town. Her name was Natalie. She had taught French in a London school and had come back to where she

was born because her marriage broke up. Her
parents bought her a woolshop. And they kept an
eye on her. Natalie and I were having dinner in a
restaurant — it was nine-thirty — and there was
her mother and father standing outside the restaurant window, smiling at us, and pointing to the
time. Next morning we were having a coffee in the
woolshop and talking about Richard Burton ... his
death was announced . . . when Natalie said, 'A
young boy, from across the street, was killed last
night in a car accident. He would always wave to
me when he went by. I won't see him again. . . . We
can't talk about him,' she said angrily. 'But we can
talk about Richard Burton and neither of us knew
him.' "

Adolphe waited for this to sink in.

"Sometimes when you see something it will
suggest something else. On the train coming
down I saw two magpies. I remembered the
rhyme.

> *One for sorrow*
> *Two for joy*
> *Three for a letter*
> *Four for something better.*

And made up this scene. There is this young
family in a train. Mother, father, young daughter.
They have just left their older son in a mental
hospital. Mother and father are tense. The young
daughter — standing at the window looking at the
passing fields — sees two magpies. She calls out
excitedly.

" 'We going to have joy. We going to have joy.' "
He hesitated.

"Of course if you have two magpies in a country
cemetery. With one bird on a gravestone and the
other on the earth beside it — you have other
possibilities.

"And if you are in this country cemetery. And
see a man, as I did, bringing flowers to the grave of
his wife. In the next scene you have that man
carrying flowers as he goes courting his new lady
friend.

"Any questions?"

There were none.

"To end this evening," Adolphe said, "Peter and I
will read you something we have written — so you
can see our credentials."

Adolphe read an amusing account about his
experiences with a dating service. "All the women
they sent were handicapped."

And I read a ten-minute story.

That night, in the goosehouse, I went to bed
with the samples of writing my lot had brought
with them. I looked forward to reading their work.
When I finished, I thought, what am I doing here?
The writing was amateurish. The prose flat, life-
less, and going all over the place. It was as if they
wanted to write and didn't know what to write
about.

We began at eight next morning. A student would
knock on the door of the goosehouse. It was
spartan but clean. I would have them sit opposite
the scrubbed wooden table. Someone had put

primroses and violets in a glass. I asked them: why did they want to write? And they talked. One student (a heavy handsome woman from Birmingham), the oldest on the course, said she was married with two small children and her husband was unemployed. Another, a small lively girl from a northern provincial town, said she was having an affair with her husband's closest friend ("He and his wife are constantly in and out of our house") and things were getting difficult. They also told me that their Teachers' Training College was closing at the end of the year. They were the last course. And none had jobs to go to when they graduated.

"Our tutor has started to write a novel."

"What will you do?"

They didn't know.

I went over their work. I showed them how to cut unnecessary words. And not to explain too much. After a few minutes they were able to do the revising themselves. I said their only responsibility — to discover their material. And gave them their first assignment. "Go outside. Describe something. So I can see it."

The last of the seven to come to the goosehouse was also the youngest on the course, Sally. A small cheerful blonde girl with a lovely smile. She had a habit of pushing her long hair away from her face. She wasn't as bad as the others but she still had some way to go. And I told her this.

"What does it matter," she said, "if someone is writing without a view of getting published. I get pleasure out of writing. I like doing it. I just want to get better. That's why I came."

I didn't understand this. I assumed that everyone who writes wants to get published. But here
was someone realistic enough, at so young an age.
Yet she couldn't stop. And neither, as I found out,
could the others.

Walking to lunch Adolphe caught up with me.
"End of our surgeries for the day," he said a little
out of breath. "I've been going non-stop. How did
yours go?"

"All right," I said, without his enthusiasm. And
told him about Sally.

He smiled. "What makes people interesting is
their dedication."

Tomorrow morning. It was Sally who came to the
goosehouse at eight. (The last person yesterday
was the first person the next.) And as it was a warm
sunny morning I suggested we have the lesson
outside.

We were sitting, quite near, at right angles. Sally
was facing the gardens. I was facing the moor.
Close by, the tall grass and bracken. Then the
distances. Areas of water, earth, sky. How timeless
and quiet. I told her that I liked her descriptions,
especially the way she described an outcrop of
granite. "As if a giant toothpaste tube had been
squeezed and the granite came out in layers, one
on top of the other." For her next assignment, I
said, I wanted her to try and trap an emotion. I was
telling her how to go about doing this when I
noticed a flash of light as the sun caught the
windscreen of a car moving on the road across the
moor. I turned my head towards Sally — her eyes

were filled with tears. I went back to the moor —
the car, like a toy, was now against the light green
then the dark green — and talked as if nothing was
happening. Sometimes I turned my head slightly
— she was still crying — and continued to talk as I
watched a kestrel hover, then glide, and turn into
the wind and hover again beating its wings without moving — in the wind — and not moving —
then still. I cut the half-hour short, said I would see
her tomorrow.

The next to come on the grass was the married
woman, Mrs Goodhand, from Birmingham. I was
more upset than I realized for I told her what
happened.

"I was sitting like this looking at the moor and
talking about writing. When, for no reason, Sally
started to cry."

I turned to look at Mrs. Goodhand. There were
tears coming down her cheeks.

"Why are you crying?"

She lowered her head and said quietly.

"Because of you."

I didn't understand. And must have shown it.
For she said,

"You're on the page."

When I saw Adolphe I told him what happened.
He wasn't surprised.

"They are reminding us we are writers."

Adolphe was taking me on one of his favourite
walks. We passed four students playing croquet on
the sunken lawn and I could hear the sound of
wood on wood as we went down a rough path

between the bracken and the gorse. Then the small fields. Butterflies were flitting around. Small light blue ones that I hadn't seen before. A light blue sea, in front, to the horizon. This immense sky. And, behind, the haunch of the moor. We walked along the curving side of a small potato field. Then another small field where the grass was high, the hedgerows full of campion, brambles, foxgloves, and primroses. We sat by a hedgerow, took our shirts off, lay on the grass facing the sun.

"You know what writers have in common?" Adolphe asked.

I didn't answer.

"A lack of confidence."

Was this true? I didn't think so. Not when I'm writing. It's when I finish something that the doubts set in.

"There are times," I said, "when I think the whole business is a confidence trick. The last time I walked into a public library it was like going into a cemetery. All those lives. All those ambitions. What does it come down to? A few books on a shelf."

I could hear a rooster crowing from the farm. And further, towards the cliffs, a working tractor.

"What else is there to do?" Adolphe said, his eyes shut. "You married?"

"Yes."

"I was. For twenty-seven years. We were married in a thunderstorm . . . just after the war . . . seems like yesterday. She now lives with someone in television. She likes celebrities. People she doesn't know. I have a housekeeper. She comes twice or three times a week. Stays the night. It's the best tonic I know."

Again we were silent.

I thought, he makes too much of being a writer. Perhaps I did too, once. But I had learned since not to make too much of anything.

"I'm a little to the left," Adolphe said. "In the thirties I was staying with an uncle in London. I went to dances. Sometimes two or three dances a night. I would pick at a lobster, at chicken done in something. Then, in the morning, walking to my uncle's house, I saw men sleeping on park benches with newspapers around their feet. I thought something wasn't right."

The sun was warm.

"Isn't this marvellous," Adolphe said, sitting up, looking at the silent view. I watched the shadow of a cloud going across the moor. As the cloud moved the light green slowly became dark green, then light green. Close to the cliffs a small fishing boat, its mizzen up. The water white in front and behind. Seagulls low over it and around its sides.

"I have led a futile life," Adolphe said. "Perhaps futile is not the right word. But it's days like the days here ... they are nothing in themselves ... but they help to give stability. I always come away, from here, feeling refreshed."

After another silence I asked him what happened after his poem was in that film.

"A lot of people came into my life. They said they wanted to look after my interests, to promote me. The phone kept ringing. I was going out to lunches, to dinners. I put on weight. I read the poem throughout the country, in town halls, in churches. It was taught in schools. I travelled. In the South of France I took a villa and stocked it with drink and food. For a while I had an enormous amount of friends.

"A few years later I wasn't news anymore. When the money ran out I did whatever I could get. Then five years ago the poetry started again. It started after a woman I loved was killed in a car crash. I kept writing. All the time waiting for it to dry up. But it wouldn't let go. I sent the poems to the magazines who published me. But that was over twenty years ago. There were new editors. They sent them back. Sometimes they came back so fast I don't think they read them. They just looked at the name. I was old hat.

"For a while I did nothing. When you live alone — there are days when you do nothing. Then I decided to send them out under another name. They were accepted. I've been doing that since. I don't write as many as I used to. Two or three a year at the most. But they get published."

"What name do you use?"

"My secret. When I have enough for a book I'll write an article for a national paper and expose it all."

The sun no longer warm. We put on our shirts and started to walk back. The estate, from below, looked like a fairy-tale castle. And what we were doing here also seemed make-believe. The students treated us as distinguished writers. They didn't know about the little articles in the provincial papers, the radio scripts, the translations. And what, I wondered, did Adolphe do for a living?

As if guessing my thoughts he said, "You know how we're going to end up. Don't you?" He was laughing. "On the street. Like those men with the newspapers." But he wasn't laughing when he said in a flat voice, "I will probably end my days alone in a rented room."

Early on the third morning the light woke me. I got up and went onto the road. It was quiet. The smell from the wild flowers. And in this light all the colours looked freshly washed. I was singing. Sometimes the road went down to a narrow valley with the earth high on either side. And sometimes the road was at the very top. And I could see for miles. Crows, rooks, gulls flew slowly over. And the occasional rabbit in the bracken.

I wasn't the only one out. I saw students, in different parts of the moor, doing the same thing.

The morning surgeries also went well. Perhaps Adolphe was right about futile days. I was becoming impatient to get back to my wife and to a short story I had been trying to write for over a year.

In the afternoon I went to see Eric Symes. He led me into a large room spotlessly clean. High ceiling, a wall-to-wall purple carpet, a piano . . . the wood shining, a comfortable settee and chairs, white walls — paintings on them. It looked like an art gallery. I recognized a Soutine, a Terry Frost, a

Peter Lanyon, Bryan Wynter, Patrick Heron, Alan Lowndes.

"I bought them, very cheaply, after the war. Afraid I'll have to sell some this year."

There were large painted dishes, with gold on the edges, propped up on the ledge above the fireplace.

"People have been very kind."

While Eric Symes was showing me around (and asked how I liked it here, and how the course was going) I could hear soft music. A pleasant woman's voice was slowly singing

> *I'll close my eyes*
> *And make believe it's you. . . .*

He walked stiffly on shaky legs, leaning on his cane, into the hall. And asked if I wanted to see upstairs. More paintings above the stairs. And, in another high room, another piano with black and white photographs propped up of a young Eric Symes. With Ivor Novello . . . with Noel Coward . . . with others, who looked vaguely familiar, in double-breasted suits and cigarettes in long cigarette holders. There were photographs of him in the costume of an Arab sheik, a Hussar, and a Foreign Legionnaire.

> *I'll close my eyes*
> *And make believe it's you. . . .*

He led me along the hall into another large and high white room. A low bed, neatly made-up, books on wooden shelves, paintings unframed on the walls. A window looked to the moor and the sea.

"Haile Selassie slept here," Eric Symes said. "He had a daughter at a school in Penzance. Before my time."

Then he led me outside. I could smell the flowers before we entered the gardens. And hear the wind. A narrow path. On either side walls of green. The path kept turning. Blue flowers, purple and white foxgloves, birds singing, slabs of granite covered in a green moss, fallen flowers on the path as well as on the trees. Clusters of red hanging, bushes of them. Some hung down from stalks, most pushed up. Delicate white-pink flowers, light-purple flowers, splashes of yellow on the green.

"I won't go through," Eric Symes said out of breath. "Follow the path. I'll see you when you come out."

The path was overhung in places by shrubs and branches of trees. I had to bend to go under. Some branches had broken and were on the ground, a light green lichen on them.

As I continued to walk, on both sides, all kinds of exotic flowers and moss and lichen. The sound of flying insects. And fallen petals, fallen flowers, decaying leaves.

When I came out Eric Symes said there were seventy-three azaleas, sixty-five different camellias, ninety-three kinds of rhododendrons. And they came from Chile, New Zealand, and other far countries.

We went back the way we came and stopped in front of the sunken lawn. There wasn't a sound. The drop of bracken and gorse; the wooden poles going down with the single cable to the small green fields, the farm, and past the farm more small fields to the cliffs. Then sea and horizon. It looked so calm.

"There's always some battle going on," Eric Symes said. "Others want to change it. I'm fighting to keep it the same. So far I've won. But they don't give up. I had to fight developers who want to build hotels. I had to fight the War Ministry. I covenanted the land to the National Trust. But I don't trust them. All it needs is some small war somewhere, with British interests, and they will have soldiers and helicopters all over the place. Sometimes there is a drought. I have to get water from the fire department. And there is always something going wrong . . . pipes, roofs, ceilings, windows, pumps. A bit of money comes from these courses. And I let it out in the summer. But not everyone likes it. They like the scenery. They can't stand the quiet or being cut off."

"What's going to happen when you're no longer here?"

"I don't know. I don't have children. I don't have family."

The effort of walking and talking had exhausted him. I thought I would leave.

"I read a lot," he said. "Send me one of your books."

On the last morning and afternoon both groups were together in the dining-room. The students read out their assignments. The others commented on them. Everyone was saying nice things. My lot wrote mostly about the different views. Adolphe's wrote about railway journeys and funerals.

In the evening there was a sense of occasion. We all washed, dressed in clean clothes. (We had caught the sun.) Adolphe looked ten years younger. The best cooks were on. Avocados with a French dressing. Roast chickens, roast potatoes, a salad. Apple pie with ice cream. And bottles of an inexpensive red wine. Everyone seemed to be in a light-hearted mood (telling us how much we had helped them, how much they got out of the course) so I thought of nothing when Adolphe came up to me with his coffee and casually said,

"When I walk out of the room the last person talking — that's the one you select."

Minutes later he called for everybody's attention.

"We have been together for four days cut off from all the things we are used to. We have got to know each other. And we have got on well. What I'm going to do is something of an experiment. I have tried it before. Sometimes it works. Sometimes it doesn't. It depends entirely on us. . . . I'm going to go out of the room. You select someone. Then I come back. And we'll see what happens."

There was some excitement. People were talking. I listened. As Adolphe went out it was Sally whose voice I heard.

"Let's pick Sally," I said.

Another student called Adolphe back.

He stood in front of us.

"The brain is a generator," he said. "It gives off electric waves. We can pick up these waves if we concentrate. Now close your eyes. And concentrate on this one person. Put everything out of your mind — just concentrate on this one person. Say that person's name in your mind. Don't think of anything else. Just concentrate. . . . Concentration is what writing is all about. . . . Put everything out of your mind. Just think of that one person."

I looked. They all had their eyes closed and their heads down as if in prayer. It was quiet.

"Someone is not concentrating," Adolphe said, his eyes shut. I closed my eyes. "That's better," he said. Another long silence. "It's getting . . . better. Yes. Yes. I'm getting something . . . it's coming through . . . it's becoming clear . . . it's Sally."

They opened their eyes. And looked surprised, pleased, excited. Adolphe was smiling.

"Shall we do it again?"

This time I picked Jimmy — a Scottish boy who was in Adolphe's class. Jimmy was sitting beside his friend Christopher.

Adolphe went through the same routine. And when he finally said Jimmy they were again surprised.

The third time he went out I said we will have Mrs Goodhand.

A student said, "You always do the picking. Why don't we pick someone?"

"It doesn't matter who does the picking," I said calmly, and asked a student to call Adolphe.

After Adolphe said Mrs Goodhand the surprise was still there though several looked puzzled and some suspicious.

We had a break to fill up with wine or coffee. The students were around Adolphe. I finally got him alone. "They're onto us," I said. "They want to pick the next one."

"Leave it to me." And walked away.

"As it is working so well," Adolphe said to everyone and smiled, "I'm going to ask Peter to go out and see if it will work with him."

I went out of the room and came back. Following Adolphe, I said, "Everyone concentrate." And I saw them close their eyes and their heads went down. The room was silent. I waited. "I'm not getting anything," I said. "Some are not concentrating." And waited for as long as I could. Then, quietly, said, "Something is starting." And waited. "Yes. Something is starting to come through. . . . I can't tell if it is a man or a woman. . . ."

I saw Christopher getting red in the face.

I quickly said, "It's becoming clear. It's Christopher."

Again the mixture of surprise and puzzlement. Except for Jimmy and Christopher who looked sideways at one another.

Next morning we were outside. (Connie had called a taxi the night before to take us to Penzance station at nine.) Adolphe was in his element. He went around in his black fedora and mustard

military coat saying, "Everything ends too soon."
Some of the girls were visibly emotional. He gave
them his address. (Only Mrs Goodhand and Sally
asked for mine.) He went off with one girl — when
they came back they were holding hands.

The taxi came. We were getting in when Eric
Symes appeared walking as fast as he could.

"The phone has been cut off."

"Why would they do that?" a student asked.

"Because I didn't pay the bill. I forgot. I forget a
lot of things. Could you," he asked Adolphe, "go to
Penzance post office and put it right?" And Eric
Symes gave Adolphe the bill and a cheque. "It's
kind of you — without the phone —"

The taxi began to move along the drive. Adolphe
was smiling and waving . . . so were the students.
"Goodbye," he called. "Goodbye. . . . Goodbye. . . ."

As soon as the taxi turned onto the road
Adolphe withdrew into his corner. We drove in
silence and looked out at the landscape.

Some miles later we were passing a granite
outcrop. It went up in horizontal layers. I could
hear Adolphe muttering to himself. "Things have
to last, to endure." About a mile later we were
driving with the road on top. The moor on both
sides of the road. And further down, to the right,
the sea and the horizon. "Once we're gone we will
be forgotten," he said. "It will be as if we have never
lived."

Then half-turning to me. "Why do we go on?"

Not waiting for a reply. "Because I have to go and
see about that telephone. You have to get back to

your wife. And who knows what we will have to do tomorrow —"

A few miles further, with St Just in the distance, he took out a folded piece of paper from his coat pocket. "A sentimental girl. I gave her my address. She gave me this." He passed the paper to me without turning his head. It was a short poem called "Volcanoes" by one of his students. Under the title she had written. "For Adolphe — who made things happen."

Outside Penzance station the taxi stopped. I got out of the car with my bag and went around to the window where he was sitting. He looked different from the person on the moor. A shabby elderly man, older than his years, with bags under his eyes.

"Now that you know my tricks the next one you'll be able to do yourself."

"Yes," I said.

He stared back at me. It became awkward. We didn't know how to say goodbye.

"The most terrible thing that can happen to a writer is success," he said in his flat voice. Then he started to smile, his face changed. "Expect a cheque in three or four weeks." He waved as the taxi drove away.

I walked into Penzance station. And the noise . . . of the trains . . . people moving . . . the clatter in the small café. . . . Even the advertisements seemed an intrusion.

GWEN JOHN

GWEN JOHN

Early in January 1984 I flew from Toronto to London. Then a train to Sheffield. My son-in-law, Kevin, met me at the railway station. And from there he drove out of the city onto moorland that led to a valley and to a stone house in Hathersage. Ellen, my eldest daughter, was having their first child. And as her mother was not alive I wanted to be there. The baby was a boy, Hugh. I stayed with them a week. Did the shopping. Helped to prepare the evening meal. (Kevin was in Chesterfield, during the day, teaching science.) Took the dog, a whippet named Gemma, out for long walks in the surrounding countryside.

It was a pleasant village, in a valley, hills all around. A few churches. A school. A short busy road. Above it, on the sloping fields, sheep. There was a butcher shop, a bakery, several fruit and vegetable stores, an Italian restaurant, some old pubs with early photographs of local cricket teams, and a good inn. It looked like a village in a children's book. The postman on his bicycle . . . the farm off the main street with working horses in the stables . . . ducks by a stream that went by a playing field . . . a small library (a room in a house) open some afternoons.

An Air Force jet appeared low overhead. Then climbed and banked quietly above the hills. I saw coaches and cars arrive with hikers and climbers. And walked in a section, up from the lowest part, where the large houses were with magnificent views of the hills. And, closer, the neatly cut bowling green with the delicate bandstand. Ellen told me that Eyam, a nearby village, was isolated in the Middle Ages because of the Black Death. People would not go in but leave food. And on a postcard (in a small newsagent post office) I read that Charlotte Brontë stayed in Hathersage, then used parts of it in *Jane Eyre*.

When it was time to leave, Kevin drove me to Chesterfield railway station. Across the moor . . . before the sun was up . . . frost was on the stubble. He went on to his school. I got on the train that arrived from the North and was going to Penzance. I couldn't see an empty seat. Everyone looked asleep. When I heard a voice say,

"You can sit beside me."

Bright, alert. She could be in her late twenties. Her black hair all over the place — probably I had woken her up. Her face was pale with dark eyes. And she wore an elegant, dark-purple, woollen suit.

"You can have the window-seat," she said. "I'm going to get some breakfast."

She came back with two fried eggs, toast, and coffee. I saw a small black case by her luggage. Perhaps a flute. After she had eaten, tidied up, we started to talk.

She had been visiting her parents in the Lake District. I told her I had just flown from Canada and was going to Cornwall.

The train was moving along. Past small fields. And, in the depressions, water. I remember the American student in the airport bus from Heathrow. In England for the first time. And excited by what he saw. "This is watercolour country," he said.

"Have you been to East Germany?"

"Yes," she said.

"How long were you there?"

"A year."

"I was there two weeks. Where were you?"

"Halle."

"I was in Halle ... a few hours ... between trains. What were you doing?"

"Teaching English."

"Did you go to Leipzig?"

"Yes."

"When I was in Leipzig I was taken to the Thomaskirche and shown where Bach played the organ. In the aisle, on the floor, there's an area of aluminum where he is buried. And in the middle of the aluminum, in large clear letters, it had B A C H. Someone had placed a red rose in a corner. The organ was at the far end of the church.

It's small. The pipes look like children's crayons standing on end."

"My boyfriend is an organist," she said. "A good one. He came to see me. We went to Leipzig. In the Thomaskirche he was given permission to play Bach's organ."

Outside. A grey sky . . . low clouds . . . small fields . . . hedges . . .

"Where are you going?"

"Oxford."

"What are you doing in Oxford?"

"A Ph.D."

"In what?"

"English."

"On what?"

"Decadence."

I thought, how marvellous. On a train in England just after eight in the morning. And we are talking about decadence.

Neither of us was certain what it was. But she was interested what form it took in art. She thought it might be when something — a way of painting, of writing, a style — goes on after the life of the original is over.

Oxford came too soon. She got off. I was on my own until St Erth where I got off, walked across the covered wooden bridge, took the branch line that went by Lelant estuary, then the coast, to St Ives.

I keep coming back. To this place. To this house. Although now it is only the top floor and the attic that I rent. I keep coming back to these shabby damp rooms, with the paintings on the walls given to me by people no longer here. The old black gas stove, the small (rust-on-the bottom) fridge, the plain wooden table. I can't leave go of this place. The life that was lived here is no longer here. The ceiling is cracked and peeling and when it rains patches are wet. The wood of some of the windows is worn and splintered. It all looks used and worn-out and not repainted or repaired. Yet I feel comfortable here even though the life wasn't comfortable. Nor is it now.

I live opposite stone — stone cottages — stone terraced houses — street after street of stone — no trees.

But there are the windows. In the rooms on the top floor. And when I go up the turning stairs to the attic. And see the colours of the far shore fields, the sun over the bay, the lighthouse, the gulls, the low clouds moving from the land to the sea.

And, from the windows, on the other side. The back and front gardens of the larger houses farther up on the slope with the neat rows of vegetables, the poppies growing wild in the tall grass, the shrubs, the flowers.

And I like being here because I'm on my own. I do what I want to do when I want to do it. I get up — the gulls wake me — before the sun is above the horizon. Make breakfast (a grilled Manx kipper), have cups of coffee, read the morning paper. Listen to the radio. For the first few days that is all I do. Except for walks by the coast, the estuary, in the country (the foxgloves), on the moor (the changing colours of the bracken), or through the town. I get fresh mackerel from the fishmonger, hot bread and saffron from the bakery. There is a familiarity . . . as if I have never been away.

But after a week, sometimes less, I am ready to leave. I've had enough. This slow pace, these uneventful days and nights, these spartan and used rooms. When I now walk through the town I see it for what it is — a backwater. A few more days . . . I feel strangely exhausted doing nothing. I go to bed, while it is still light, draw the curtains. And it's as if I'm in a small cabin, on a large passenger ship, on an ocean. The ship has its engines stopped. And it's drifting.

Gradually the pace that is here takes over. The tiredness goes. I go upstairs to the attic, to this familiar desk, and start to write.

I remain here, living like this, until I finish something, or a first draft of it. Then I fly back to Toronto where I live a different life with Mrs Garrens, a widow of forty-six. She has a large secluded house in three acres of grounds (lawns, gardens, trees), a gardener, a housekeeper. In winter we travel.

So these two lives. The one with Mrs Garrens began four years ago — eighteen months after her husband, an industrialist, died. The one in St Ives, in 1949, when I was twenty-four and living in London for the first time.

There was still food rationing, bomb damage, cigarettes under the counter, *The Third Man*, cheap Algerian wine, large Irish sausage at Sainsbury's. And a lot of displaced people.

I had come over to do postgraduate work at the University of London and rented two rooms above

the Institute of Child Psychology in Notting Hill
Gate. Opposite was a garage. The door beside the
garage had *Theosophy* painted above it.

In my third week, I returned late from a party
and couldn't get the key to open the outside door.
I saw a light in the garage. And walked across the
street. A bare bulb from the ceiling and a thin man
in a white shirt, in his sixties, was reading a news-
paper and smoking a cigarette.

I told him I lived above the Institute and couldn't
get in.

He remained silent. Then said.

"Come with me."

I followed him in the dark to the back of the
garage where cars were parked.

"You want a Rolls or a Bentley?"

"Bentley," I said.

He opened the boot of a car, brought out a
blanket, unlocked a back door, put the light on,
gave me the blanket, and said goodnight.

It was all white inside. A shiny white, like satin. I
stretched out across the back seat. It was like being
in an expensive coffin.

When I woke it was raining. And almost nine
next morning.

That evening I went to Chelsea to see Nicholas
Kempster who was with me at university and lived
in a bed-sit on Oakley Street. He left a note on the
door saying he'd be back in a few hours.

I went to wait in the nearest pub. It was dark and
gloomy (the walls were painted brown) and empty
except for an old man sitting by the side of the
fireplace. He seemed to be staring into space. A

pint of beer was on a small table in front of him. He didn't touch it all the time I was there. He had on an officer's fawn greatcoat, unbuttoned. His hair was grey and uncombed. I recognized him as Augustus John.

The next time I saw Augustus John was two years later, in a black and white photograph on the wall of a pub, The Globe, in Penzance. The others in the photograph were Maurice Mayfield (a war artist) and his attractive wife, Nancy, dressed like a gypsy. Maurice Mayfield tried to look and live like Augustus John. I knew this because, in those two years, I met Elizabeth. We married. And decided to come down to Cornwall. We rented a large granite house with a walled garden from Maurice Mayfield. When he heard what I was doing he let me have it cheaply.

So we lived in this fine large house (it was the finest house we ever lived in) while the owner and his wife and four young children lived in a small primitive cottage on the moors. Maurice would come in every morning on an old bicycle to his studio — a small partitioned section of the building, near the house, where I worked. He always wanted me to see his new paintings. They were of peasant or gypsy women. Stylized figures, often in black, like the one above our bed called "The Angel of Sleep." Though I didn't care for his work, I liked Maurice. Years later, I was told he came from a working-class family by the London docks. You wouldn't have known from the way he spoke. The soft voice, the careful diction, the good manners. A

large man with a small head, short red hair, blue
eyes, a face that looked as if he had just caught the
sun. He went around dressed like a peasant
farmer. And he smiled easily.

He told me he was trying a new technique (bees
wax) and wanted me to see what he had done. I
didn't like any of them. Then I saw on the wall a
small unframed oil of a woman's head and shoulders. She wasn't smiling. The hair was close to her
head, parted in the middle and pulled back, to
form a bun. She didn't have much of a chin. It was
mostly in browns. But there was an immediacy, a
human quality, that none of the others had.

"I like that," I said. Glad that here was something
I could be enthusiastic.

"It's not by me," Maurice smiled. "It's by Gwen
John."

It was the first time I had heard her name.

At Mousehole we lived on the slope of a hill in this
cut-granite house, with the high granite wall
around it, and the copper beech, bamboos, roses,
inside. At night, in bed, we could see the roofs of
the cottages sloping to the harbour. The boats, in
the bay, fishing between the chimneys. We had
little money. I went out with the fishermen from
Newlyn. And bicycled back after midnight . . . the
moon on the water . . . heard a fox . . . an owl from
Paul. Then going up the outside granite steps
wondering if we still had electricity. Two days later
an elderly man, from the electricity company,
came to disconnect our supply. I held the ladder so
he could climb and do it.

That night we ate our meal by candlelight.

The fishermen left pilchards and mackerel outside the front door. The farmer, from the fields above, left broccoli, new potatoes, and lettuce. Ellen was born. The butcher, Mr. Brewer, left five shillings on her pram when she was asleep. Then the money ran out and there was little I could do here to earn any. So we moved: to London, Devon, Brighton. When things improved we went back to Cornwall and to this house.

A few years later I read that Augustus John had died. And on the television news caught a glimpse of Maurice Mayfield at the funeral. Then Maurice Mayfield died. Our children left home. Elizabeth died. I went back to Canada, to Toronto, where I met Mrs Garrens.

It started as a business arrangement. Mr Garrens had left instructions that he didn't want a memorial stone. But Mrs Garrens wanted to do something. She told me he liked books and thought of having a book prize, in his name, to be given every two years to a promising writer. And she wanted me to select the writer. We continued to meet in her house to discuss this. Soon we talked about other things. The prize was never mentioned. We were both still young enough to miss the physical side of marriage. And we didn't like living on our own.

But I have this illness. What other men do with other women I can only do with my wife. And when she died I thought, now I have to learn to be promiscuous.

When I moved in with her it was Mrs Garrens's life that I began to live. Not only the house with the spacious grounds. But the large rooms with floor to wall white carpets, the walls painted a delicate green. The paintings on the walls. The one I liked was a drawing, a nude, by Matisse. The meals cooked by the housekeeper. The dinner parties. I also began to travel.

She took me first to France. (Mrs Garrens grew up in the South of France and talked about the fields of blue cornflowers in the long grass that were part of her childhood.) I had never been to France. It was the country Elizabeth always wanted to see.

In Paris we stayed in a hotel by the Luxembourg Gardens. We often went into the Gardens. Then to a restaurant, then back to the hotel. We went to Marseille and did the same. We both seemed to have a lot of energy, especially early in the morning, as if we had to catch up on lost time. She would make a sound from her throat as she reached her climax. Then give me these quick little kisses all over my face.

At breakfast, she said,

"Your eyes go up when you're happy."

Next morning at breakfast she said,

"Your eyes tilt when you come."

On our last day in Marseille she asked,

"Is there any place you would like to see?"

I said Dieppe.

So we went to Dieppe. Went for walks by the coast. Had picnics in the countryside. And to a different restaurant every night. And sometimes we ate in the hotel where we stayed along the front. The bed was wide and high. And there were long mirrors on the doors of the wardrobe.

"I'm your last fuck," Mrs Garrens said.

That's the way our life has gone. And I like the life we have together. But after seven or eight months, I become restless. Another month or two and I need to leave. I am pulled back (why I don't know) to this pretty backwater, these seedy rooms, to being alone. And to work here.

This January I told Mrs Garrens.

"I need to go to St Ives."

Mrs Garrens doesn't like this. When I tell her I need to go she becomes anxious. We have little quarrels. And when I'm packed, the bags downstairs, waiting for the limousine to come up the drive to take me to the airport, I feel sad about leaving her.

We sit in the front room, having a drink and talking quietly.

She never uses my name but calls me you.

And I always call her Mrs Garrens.

I arrived back here on January 10th. There had been continual rain in England for weeks. Drizzle. The sky was overcast. It was raining now. And in the passing small fields there was flooding.

When I arrived in St Ives it was grey and wet. The open railway station above the beach was deserted. I began to walk with my bags. The streets were empty. Just the sound of the gulls. The rooms, the attic, were cold. They were damp. There was no heat except from the gas rings of the black kitchen stove. I put the three on that were working. There was also a strike. The water was cut off. When it came on I was told to fill the bath. I would take saucepans of water from the bath to the kitchen, to make coffee, to wash the dishes, to shave.

I had caught a cold and had a temperature. I decided to go to bed. But I wanted something to read. I went to the small library. Saw a biography by Susan Chitty of Gwen John. I returned to the cold damp and dusty rooms, put on two sweaters, thick woollen socks, and several extra blankets. I went to bed, in the narrow front bedroom, with the bottle of duty-free brandy that I had bought.

And began to read.

How Gwen John led a middle-class upbringing in Wales. Went to Paris to be a painter. Became a model to earn some money. Met Rodin. They became lovers. She was, for a while, happy. Then he discarded her. She wrote him letters every day. And waited in Luxembourg Gardens hoping to get a glimpse of him.

After that she withdrew . . . she continued to paint . . . but didn't look after herself . . . hardly eating . . . little money . . . she ended up in a shed at the bottom of a garden . . . the rain coming in from the roof.

The Second World War. The Germans invaded France. Augustus John was in the south of France with some of his women friends and several children. He was to drive and pick up Gwen John in Paris. Then head to one of the ports. But he avoided Paris. And got on the last ship for England.

With the Germans invading, Gwen John left Paris. Got as far as Dieppe. Collapsed in the street. People thought she was a vagrant. Took her to a hospice. Where she died. No one knows where she is buried. Augustus John was supposed to do a memorial stone. But he never got around to it. . . .

SOAP OPERA

SOAP OPERA

I phoned my mother in Ottawa just after 6 P.M. No reply. A few minutes later I tried again. Then I took Fred, mostly beagle, out for his walk . . . through the small park . . . (at twelve he still has this rapid acceleration and expects me to throw a tennis ball for him to chase) . . . around the reservoir and the wall of green trees that hide the ravine. In front, by the path, were the four saplings planted a few years ago with the name-plates: *In Memory of My Beloved Papa Joseph Podobitko*. I wondered who Joseph Podobitko was. I had asked the Portuguese gardener, who looked after the grounds, if Joseph Podobitko had worked here. He told me that Joseph Podobitko didn't work here. He didn't know who he was, and it cost three hundred dollars to put up one of those saplings.

I came back to the house with Fred and phoned again. I tried the Civic Hospital. I asked if she was a patient. Silence. Then her voice (slow and shaky) said,

"Hello."

"When did you go in?"

"This morning at ten." It was an effort for her to talk. "I'm just played out."

"I'll see you tomorrow," I said. "I'll take the early train."

That evening I phoned my sister Sarah in Carleton Place. She had come to Ottawa and had been staying with mother for a week.

"I couldn't take it any more," Sarah said. "She doesn't want to live. She has given up."

"A person who calls an ambulance and gets herself admitted as an emergency case hasn't given up."

"But you don't know what she talks about."

"I'll take the early train," I said. "It gets in around noon."

"I'll be with her in the morning and you will be with her in the afternoon."

"Yes," I said. "We'll get together later."

My mother was on the fifth floor of the surgical ward in a room by herself. When I walked in she was asleep, propped up by pillows. I was dismayed at how she had changed. I brought one of the grey leather chairs to the side, sat, and waited.

It was a large air-conditioned room with two windows. The blinds were half-way down, the curtains half-way across. On a small table, by the bed, a telephone. On a chest of drawers some flowers wished her a speedy recovery. On the wall a painting, a reproduction, of two rowing boats by a blue pier with the moon out. The room had another room within it. A private bathroom. All the walls were orange and cream. And the doors light blue. The large front door was opened as far as it could go. And on it a name-plate: *Donated by Mr Thomas Sachs.*

She opened her eyes.

"Hello, mother."

"Have you been here long?"

"No. It's a nice large room."

"I paid into Blue Cross," she said weakly, "for semi-private. But they put me in here. Do you think they made a mistake?"

"I wouldn't think so."

She looked up at the two standing metal forms beside her. One had a bag that was giving her blood. It was almost empty. The other, water. And that was full. She watched closely, as I did, as the drops appeared.

"What did the doctor say?"

"That I have jaundice. That I'm bleeding inside. But they say they can stop that. He's a very nice man."

"Was Sarah here in the morning?"

"Yes."

"How is Sarah?"

"Hysterical. She looks at me and laughs. Then she cries."

We were silent. "Help me up."

I put my hand behind her back and eased her forward. I was surprised at the thickness of the spine, how much it protruded, and how light she was. She sat, with her head down, as if waiting for strength to return.

"I can't eat," she said in despair.

There were small cardboard containers on the table by her bed. "Would you like this?" It was prune juice. "This one?" Orange juice. "This?" A white-purple thing labelled *Ensure*. She answered by an almost imperceptible movement of her head. I put in a stubby straw, bent it near the top, and held the *Ensure* while she sipped it all. Then she reached, slowly, for the box of Kleenex on her bed and, carefully, dried the corners of her mouth.

Again we were silent.

"You will stay in the apartment?"

"Yes."

With a finger she pointed to the dresser by the wall. I opened the top drawer and saw a large beige purse.

"Take the keys . . . Have you got the keys?"

I showed them to her.

"In the fridge . . . help yourself. There is coffee. Eat whatever you like. You have my permission."

"I'll water the plants."

"It would be better if I didn't have them."

"How much water do you give?"

"Not too much. Every two or three days."

"Anything you want me to bring?"

"The small key is for the mail-box. . . . See if any mail. In the dining-room . . . in the drawer . . . are two cheques. Six hundred dollars and something. Take the bank-book . . . pay in my account."

I said I would.

She wanted to be eased back to the way she had been.

"Mrs Tessier, across the hall, takes in *The Citizen*. Tell her you are in the apartment and you will have the paper. I have paid three months in advance ... I don't think I'll go back there. I'll go to some other place for a rest."

The large blue eyes. The grey hair, usually neatly combed up, was loose on the sides. She did not have her teeth in and her mouth looked small. I thought of her independent nature, the quick intelligence, and how she coped with things.

"I'm all played out," she said. "But I'm not tired of living."

She watched the blood and the water drip.

"It's working," I assured her.

But she continued to watch.

"Another doctor came," she said. "A young doctor. He asked me questions about my operations. He said I had some kind of anaemia that only Jews from East Europe have. Did you know about that?"

"No."

"He said the mother passes it to her siblings. Does that mean daughters?"

"Sons and daughters."

We were silent.

"Do you want to see anyone?"

She said no with her head.

"If anyone phones. If anyone in the building asks. Say I have gone in the hospital for tests. Don't say anything more. Just tests."

"Yes."

Again we were silent.

"I'm going to close my eyes now," she said.

The closed eyes made the socket bones more visible. Faint sunlight was on her face and on the far wall. I knew nothing of her life in Poland except what she told me. "I liked a young man, a red-head. He was a scholar. My mother and father didn't think he could make a living. . . . At my wedding they threw money in pails. . . . We had a large house and a servant. When I was coming to Canada she begged me to take her." Then the difficult early years in Ottawa that she doesn't want to be reminded of. And for the last twenty-one years on her own, in a senior citizens' building, opposite a small park. I thought again of her generous nature, how independent she was, and how she came out with unexpected things.

Her eyes opened.

"I need a bed-pan," she said in a low voice.

A white flex, with a white button on it, was held to one of the pillows by a safety pin. I picked up the flex and pressed the button. A snapping sound and a slight electric shock.

"When the nurse comes I'll go," I said. "And I'll come tomorrow. Sarah said she would be here as well."

I went over and kissed her on the forehead.

"With jaundice I don't think you should kiss."

I opened the door of her apartment. In the half-light I could see the three small rooms. Brought the suitcase in, quickly drew the curtains, and opened the windows. All the clocks had stopped.

The place looked as if it was left in a hurry. In the kitchen, dishes on the draining-board were upside down. In the bedroom the large bed was not made. A dress was on the back of the rocking-chair. Two-tone, beige and brown shoes were under the bed. The calendar, by the window, had not been changed in two months.

She had kept everything neat and clean. Now a thin layer of dust was on the furniture and on the wooden floor. And on the leaves of the plants in the front room. The earth was dry. I watered the plants. Looked in the fridge. A few potatoes were sprouting. The pears were bruised and had started to go rotten. I couldn't understand why Sarah hadn't tidied up. There was some half-used cottage cheese, a bottle of apple juice, a tin of *Ensure*. The cupboard, by the sink, was packed with tins as if for a siege. I made a cup of coffee, brought it into the front room, sat by the table, and started to relax.

I had not been here on my own before. How small and still. And full of light. The chesterfield set, from the house, was too large. She brightened the settee with crocheted covers — bands of red, yellow, green — that kept slipping down. And cushions with embroidered leaves of all kinds. The same was on the chair, by the side of the window, overlooking the street and the small park. (The Lombardy poplars are gone. But the gazebo is there. And kids throwing a ball around.) On the other side of the window, against the wall, a large black and white television was on the floor. No longer working. Its use, to support the plants on its top. Beside it: the glass-enclosed wooden cabinet with her best dishes, best cups, saucers, the Chinese plate that goes back to my childhood, the Bernard Leach mugs and bowl that I brought back on visits from St Ives. On top of the cabinet a family tree. Small, round, black and white photographs in metal frames hung from metal branches. Father and mother, in the park by the river, some fifty years ago. Sarah and I . . . when we were around ten and eight . . . the people we married . . . our children . . . with their husbands . . . their children . . .

The room's centre piece was the nickel-plated samovar. On the long wooden dresser, against the far wall, with the mirror above it. Two silver candlesticks were on either side. A brass pestle and mortar. A silver tray. And more plants, lots of them, just leaves in various shapes and sizes.

Above the settee, two small paintings of people at the Wailing Wall. Beside it a framed diploma-looking paper with a red seal at the bottom.

First Distinguished Service Award
Presented to
The Dedicated Men and Women
Past and Present of
The Ottawa Burial Society

"What do you do?"
"Sew shrouds."
I said nothing.
"It's an honour," she said indignantly. "Not everyone gets asked."

On the wall, a watercolour of St Ives (signed Holland). It was done from the Malakoff, overlooking the harbour, before TV aerials were on the cottages. I grew up, in Ottawa, with this watercolour. And in all those years we didn't know what it was. In 1949 I left for England. Five years later I made my first visit back. Paid the taxi, walked into the house, kissed them, and saw the watercolour.

"That is where I live in England."

No reaction from either of them.

The phone rang.

"Hello."

"Annie?"

"No, it's her son."

"Where's your mother?"

"In hospital."

"Not again. What is it this time?"

"They don't know. She has gone in for tests."

The telephone was loud. I had to hold it away.

"Who shall I say phoned?"

"Tell her that Phyllis Steinhoff called. We belong to the Golden Age Club. We go and play bingo together."

"I'll tell her."

Silence.

"Your mother is a lovely woman. She is intelligent. And she is nice."

I went to the door, directly opposite in the hall, and knocked. Mrs Tessier, small, gentle, dumpy, with brown eyes and glasses, opened the door. She always looked cheerful.

"Hello Mrs Tessier. I came because my mother is in hospital."

"How is your mother?"

"Not well."

"What is wrong?"

"They don't know. She is in for tests."

"You want the paper?"

"Yes."

She disappeared.

"You want the others?"

"No, just today's."

"How long you here?"

"Two or three days."

"I hope your mother comes home soon."

I decided to change the bed linen. The linen cupboard was packed tight with neatly folded sheets, pillow-cases, and towels. I was taking out a couple of pillow-cases when I saw a used brown envelope. It was unsealed. Inside were dollar bills. Twenties, tens, fives, twos and ones. I counted. It came to a hundred and eighty dollars. When I took out the sheets I saw more used brown envelopes, unsealed, also with money. I counted all the money. It came to $2,883.00. I put my hand between other sheets, pillow-cases, towels. No more envelopes but a small battered cardboard box held together by red elastic bands. Inside, large silver coins that I remembered as a child. A double eagle on one side, two heads on the other. She had brought them over with the samovar, the candlesticks, the pestle and mortar, the silver tray.

It was humid and hot. I had a bath. Then phoned Sarah. She was staying with her daughter Selina and her family on the outskirts. I asked Sarah if she knew about the money.

"Yes."

"Do you know how much there is?"

"No."

"Two thousand eight hundred and eighty-three dollars."

"It's for her funeral. She told me what to do when she dies. I have to call Pettigorsky from the burial society right away. She wants no autopsy. The coffin must be the Jewish way. No nails. Shiva she wants private. At her place. Only the family. And she wants me to get someone to say Kaddish for her. I'll pay him from that money."

"She hasn't mentioned any of this to me."

"When I'm with her that's all she talks about."

Next day I walked to the bank on Rideau near the market and paid the government cheques into her account. Then to the Rideau Centre, got on a bus to the hospital. Sarah was sitting in a leather chair by the bed. Mother was asleep. She was having another blood transfusion. The water was dripping as well. Sarah saw me. "Hi," she said and smiled. We both walked quietly over and kissed.

"How is she?"

"Most of the time she sleeps."

"Has the doctor been?"

"Yes."

"What did he say?"

"He said, 'We are not going to let your mother die.' "

We were silent.

"She doesn't have cancer," Sarah said.

Another silence.

"Why didn't she keep the money in the bank?"

Mother opened her eyes.

"I couldn't put the money in the bank," she said slowly. "If I did I would have to pay more rent."

I sat her up. Got some juice and a straw. She didn't have the strength to hold it. When she finished and wiped her lips she said, "It is not necessary to put this in a story."

"I only write about people I like."

She wasn't convinced.

"Phyllis Steinhoff phoned," I said.

"You didn't tell her anything."

"That you were having tests."

Silence.

"And Dinka called," I said.

"Is she in Ottawa?"

"Yes, for the weekend. Do you want to see her?"

"No," she said quietly.

We were silent again.

"How old is Dinka?"

"She is four years older than me and she runs around like a girl."

"Did she marry again?"

"She did. But she asked him to leave."

Another silence.

"In your letter-box," I said, "you had a notice saying that men are coming next week to clean your windows."

"No," she said. "I don't want anyone to go in there. It's dirty. Write on a piece of paper Mrs Miller doesn't want her windows washed. Then stick the paper, with tape, on the outside of the door. You get the tape in the dresser of the living-room."

Another silence.

She wanted to be eased back, propped up by the pillows. I suggested to Sarah that as I'm here she might like a break and have coffee in the cafeteria.

When Sarah left I told mother what was in the news. "Waldheim was elected President of Austria." She looked surprised. "The Blue Jays are not doing so good. It's their pitching." I showed her photographs of St Ives that I took on my last visit. "Do you remember that summer . . . the two weeks you were there?"

"It was the best holiday I had."

"You used to walk along the beach and pick the small pink shells at the tideline."

"I still have them."

We were silent.

"I'm going to close my eyes now," she said.

When Sarah came we went out in the corridor.

"What else did the doctor say?"

"That she still has jaundice. Why they don't know. He said they were thinking of doing an operation to find out. She is all for it. I don't want to go on like this, she said, if they can do anything — let them do it." But they think she is a poor risk and wouldn't survive. She's not eating."

A nurse came and woke her to take a sample of blood. I told Sarah I would go to the waiting-room at the end of the corridor.

On the way I saw a young doctor.

"They took a piece of her liver," I said.

"When was that?"

"On Friday. How long will it take?"

"The pathologists are in a class by themselves. They take their time."

"I guess we'll just have to wait."

"I don't think whatever they find will make much difference."

In a room with the door open I saw a nurse by the bed of a patient. A tube was being shoved down her throat.

"Let me die."

"Swallow it, dear, as if it is a piece of bread."

"Let me die."

"I'm not allowed to. Now swallow it for me, dear, as if it is a piece of bread."

I returned to my mother's room.

"Selina is coming in a half-hour," Sarah said, "to pick me up for supper. She's invited you as well."

"You'll go," mother said.

She knew I didn't want to.

Whenever I arrived from Toronto to see her. And after we had eaten and had a talk, she would say, "Call up Sarah. Call up Selina."

I said nothing.

"Do it for me."

Selina had been in Toronto for two days at a real-estate conference. (She is high up in the company.) And was coming from the airport to the hospital. We were walking, from the hospital, to Selina's car when Selina stopped.

"She's going to die."

"Yes," I said.

Selina was Sarah's only child. A tall pale woman with blonde hair, a small face, a nice smile, blue eyes. She looked pretty but anaemic. And there was a toughness about her. The few times I did go to their house she inevitably forced a confrontation.

She had tried teaching, advertising. But she hadn't found what she was good at until she went into real-estate. She was married to George (he was fourteen years older) who smoked a pipe, worked in the Civil Service, and spoke in a slow, deep voice. They lived in a large new house, in a windswept field, on a housing estate near a lake. The nearest place, Rockliffe, was some ten miles away. Their son, Scott, had his mother's eyes and complexion. But looked oddly serious. "He's very clever," my mother told me. Then, lowering her voice as if she was going to tell me something she shouldn't, "He's a genius." Scott's favourite reading was stocks and shares. But at twelve he wasn't allowed to play the market. I once asked him if he played sports. "Football," he said. "What position?" "Centre forward — I'm very good."

I don't remember the meal. It was afterwards — when we went into the large sitting-room with the Eskimo carvings, the Indian paintings — that Selina started.

"This is the first time for you. All the other years you weren't here. We had to take her to the hospital. See her through the operations. While you were away in England."

"You're lucky," I said. "You know her in a way that I don't."

An awkward silence.

"Why did you go away?" Selina said.

"I had to."

"You didn't have to. You could have stayed and got a job in the government."

"I had to leave," I said. "The family doctor told me to get away."

"Why would he say a thing like that?"

"Because of her," I said. "He told me to get as far away from home as possible. She was too strong. She dominated the rest of the family. Because she could do things well she wouldn't let anyone else do anything. I saw what she did to father. And he was devoted to her. She was trying to do the same to me." I stopped from saying — and look what she did to Sarah.

Then George said, "When you come on a visit she doesn't want us to know you are in Ottawa."

Another silence.

"Selina thinks we should sit Shiva here," Sarah said.

"What's wrong with her apartment?"

"It's too small," Selina said. "Three people in there and there's no room to move."

"But here — it's miles from anywhere."

All the people who would come," George said, "have cars."

I thought I knew what was not being said. My mother's apartment was not only small it was in a senior citizen's place. And I could see it was no longer going to be private, a small family thing, but a social occasion.

"I'll be here for the funeral," I said. "But I won't sit Shiva."

"Why not?" Sarah shouted. "It's therapy."

"I don't believe in it."

"But for Ma."

"To remember someone," George quietly said to Sarah, "you don't have to sit Shiva."

He had, on marrying Selina, converted to being a Jew.

"You don't have any feeling for this family." Selina was angry. "You just don't have it."

In my mother's apartment I couldn't go to sleep. I finished reading *The Citizen*. There were no books. Only those I gave her that she kept hidden, in the bedroom, in drawers. They were in mint condition signed to my father and to her. Then only to her. She is the only one in the family who reads my things.

I was looking for a photograph of my father — a studio photograph, of how he looked before he came to Canada — and couldn't find it. But I did find a glass jar with the small pink shells that she collected on the beach in St Ives. And faded cuttings — from *The Journal* and *The Citizen*, of my early books — that I had forgotten. Some large boxes of chocolates unopened. Horoscopes that she cut from the paper. (Sarah was also an Aries.) A flyer that said, "Your psychic portrait rendered by the combined skills of an astrologist and of an artist. Strategically placed in your home, it allows for meditation on self, and to work out one's destiny." And it gave two telephone numbers.

In her clothes closet, at the bottom, large leather purses. Brown, beige, black. And none looked used. Inside they had loose change and a wrapped toffee or two. There were small yoghurt containers filled with pennies. One had American pennies. The others Canadian. Some were bright as if newly minted. I saw a small hand-mirror. The glass was cracked. I remember it because of the black and white drawing on the back — a woman's face and neck and dense black hair. I last saw it as a child on her dresser in the bedroom. Now, the drawing didn't look right. I turned the hand-mirror upside down. The drawing became another drawing. A woman had her hand in her pubic hair. I felt an intruder. I didn't want to look anymore.

Next morning I walked to Rideau Street and to the Rideau Bakery. On visits I always drop in to buy some bread. I bought a rye, to take back to Toronto, when one of the owners came in from the back. (We both went to York Street School.) He was talking to a well-dressed woman when he saw me.

"Going to see your mother?"

"Yes."

"This is Mrs Miller's son," he introduced me to Mrs Slover, a furrier's wife.

"Your mother," said Mrs Slover, "is a very nice person." Then looking directly at me. "Are you a nice person?"

"No," I said.

"Give her my regards when you see her. She is a lovely lady." And walked quickly away.

The owner of the Rideau Bakery looked confused.

"And remember me to your mother," he said quickly.

"She is in hospital," I said.

She was asleep when I entered her room. There was only the drip. I went out, in the corridor, towards the reception desk, when I met the surgeon. A stocky man, with glasses, from Newfoundland. He was in-between operations. They were, he said, still trying to find out why she wasn't eating. I told him I had someone coming from England. Would it be all right if I went back to Toronto. How long would I be away? About five days. He hesitated. "That should be all right."

I returned to the room. When she opened her eyes I gave her some *Ensure*. And said I would be going to Toronto as Henry, a friend from St Ives, was due tomorrow evening. I'd stay the weekend. And be back to see her the following week.

"The surgeon has my phone number."

"Did you have a nice time at Selina's?"

"Yes."

We remained silent.

"I'm going to close my eyes now."

After she woke, I said I would leave as I wanted to pack and close the apartment.

On the open front door I saw the name-plate.

"Who is Mr Thomas Sachs?"

"A bachelor," she said.

In the Union Station, waiting for Henry to arrive, I am early and having a coffee. And think how lucky I was to have grown up with painters. Painters are much more open than writers. They seem to enjoy their work more — more extrovert. And Henry was like that. When I first knew him he and his wife Kath were working in a café opposite Porthmeor Beach. And Henry painted when he could. He had one of the studios (large, spartan) facing the Beach. And let me use it. The tall end-windows (that looked out on sand, surf, the hovering gulls) had a wide window-sill. I had my typewriter on the sill and wrote while Henry painted behind me. I could hear him talking to himself. "Look at that green. . . . That red sings. . . ." And when the work was going he would sing quietly: "Life is just a bowl of cherries." Just that line. And when a painting was finished he wanted me to see it. I said I liked it. "But it is so still. Quiet."

"All good paintings," he said, "have a feeling of calm about them."

Henry began to paint in Germany as a prisoner-of-war. "I got canvas from the pillow-cases. Oil from the odd tin of sardines." He also went hungry. After the war he married. Left a struggling working-class home, in the provinces, to come to St Ives. He had a thing about those who were (like us) in St Ives but who had private incomes or parents with money. This didn't bother me. I guess you have to be English to have this love-hate with class. I remember when one of our lot (money behind him) won a prize for one of his paintings. We met in the pub by the parish church and the

War Memorial garden. He bought Henry and me a beer.

When we left the pub Henry was angry.

"A half-pint of bloody beer. Christ, if I'd won that money I'd have bought everyone double whiskies."

After that summer, and those early years, we moved apart. I heard he was teaching in an art school near London. I read about his exhibitions in the paper. Sometimes I saw him, briefly, in London. It was still a struggle.

More years passed.

Then in the spring of 1980 I came to Toronto. I was living in a modest high rise in Yorkville. When Henry phoned. He was in Toronto. He had flown from Alberta and was on his way back to England. Could I come to this restaurant and join him for dinner.

The taxi brought me to a seedy street near Kensington Market. I went up a narrow worn-out staircase. Turned into a barn-like room. Lots of tables. No customers. A man was behind a small bar by the wall near the door. A woman, in a simple all-black dress, came towards me. I asked for Henry. She led me through a door to a room in the back.

It was all red. The wallpaper was a deep red. Red lights were on the walls. The tablecloths were red. The small lights, on the tables, had red lampshades. There was only one person in the room. Henry, sitting by a large red table and smiling.

"It's a brothel," he said.

We had a platter of seafood. We drank and talked. About our friends, our children, and what we had been doing. He had been a guest lecturer at Banff for two months. Things, he said, were beginning to pick up. But he still had to hustle.

After the meal we went into the other room, stood at the bar, drank with the proprietor and his wife. Neither could speak much English. She was telling me that her husband played football for Portugal when a slight man, in a light-grey summer suit, joined us. He must have had his meal somewhere in the large room. But we didn't notice. He said he was an American. After a while he said he worked for the CIA. Still later, Henry and the CIA man began to dance. I danced with the proprietor's wife. Then we all put our arms over the shoulder of the person on either side. The proprietor joined us. And we moved around the empty restaurant as a chorus line. Henry singing "Life is just a bowl of cherries."

Out in the street we asked the CIA man where he was staying. The Windsor Arms. So we walked to the nearest main road and waited for a taxi to drive by. The grey light of early morning. It was cold and shabby. A gusty wind. Loose newspapers. And no cars. The CIA man began to take out dollar bills from his jacket pockets and threw them up into the air. The wind blew them away. Henry and I went after the loose bills . . . on the road . . . the sidewalk . . . across the street . . . and stuffed them back into the man's pockets. Then he took them out again and threw them in the air.

And again we went after them. . . . Until a taxi finally came along.

Since then Henry has called that night magical. A word I never use.

This time he had flown from England to New York. Spent four days looking at galleries and museums. Then took the train to Toronto.

"It's marvellous," he said in the taxi. "I don't have to lecture or teach or flog my paintings. I can do just what I want to do. Enjoy myself. And I have enough money not to pinch and scrape. From here, I'll go to Vancouver. See *Expo*. Then fly back."

He liked Fred. I showed him his room. We both got dressed up. Henry in a light blue silk jacket, a silk shirt, light blue trousers, a black beret.

"How's your Mum?"

"Dying."

"She knows you know," he said.

Henry is tall and stocky with a grey moustache and glasses. A woman I know, who saw us walking down Yonge Street, phoned up after he had gone and asked, "Who was that policeman you were with?"

We were having a drink before going out. His eldest son was acting in the West End in a Stoppard play. His youngest was studying languages in Munich. "And playing cricket for the MCC."

"I didn't know he was that good."

"The Munich Cricket Club. After a game if he's done well he will phone. If he doesn't phone I know he didn't get many runs."

It is only after we have told each other about our families that we get onto work.

"I've never been so busy," Henry said. "I can barely cope. I think it's to do with age. It is so strange to be so busy that there is never a minute to spare. Not until I sit down in the evening and fade out in front of the TV. I can hardly believe it. My early work continues to sell. I am so confused. I don't know whether to stop letting the last few things go or just treble the prices."

The taxi arrived.

He was excited.

"Where are we going?"

The taxi stopped on a badly lit street by some garbage. There was an open door, a worn-out staircase.

Henry was smiling. "It's the same place."

There was the man and the woman. They said they remembered us. I don't know if they did. The front barn of a room had no customers. We asked if we could go to the back. She said, in poor English, it was closed.

We sat, by a table, against a wall. And all those white laid-out empty tables stretched in front of us.

The proprietor sat in front of a large TV screen. It was raised and could be seen all over the room. Benny Hill was chasing some girls who kept dropping their clothes.

The woman in the black dress came to take our order. In a firm but friendly voice Henry said, "We'll have champagne."

The woman went away.

Henry looked relaxed and happy.

She returned to say no champagne.

"No champagne," Henry said. "Bloody hell."

"Last night a wedding. No champagne."

He looked upset.

"Shall we have a Scotch?"

"Yes," I said.

She went away.

We were silent.

"You know," Henry said, "I wanted to come and see you. Go to a restaurant. And just say: We'll have champagne. I remember at The Tinners . . . I was strapped for money . . . I was nursing a half-pint of bitter. . . . When in walked John Friel. And it was the way he said, in that arrogant plummy voice of his, a bottle of champagne. I thought, someday I'm going to do that."

We started with Portuguese sardines.

I told him that last summer I went to Paris and Marseille with a woman who opened up France for me. And it was in a small fishing place near Marseille, called Cassis, where I had the best sardines.

"I was in Marseille," he said, "before France fell. I was in the cavalry. We went to a brothel. There were three of us. All young. We kept coming back. They began to charge us hardly anything. They were glad to see us. I wondered why."

"Did you come back to the same girl?"

"Yes," he said. "I decided that they had two-way mirrors. They made their money from those who watched my ass going up in the air."

"Did you like the girl?"

"Oh yes," he said. "I liked her."

Next night I took him to an Italian restaurant, on St
Clair West, where I knew the food was good and
Henry said he liked Italian food. And the same
thing happened. He asked for champagne. The
proprietor, who was our waiter, looked sullen.
He came back with a bottle of Asti Spumante.
"I don't believe it," Henry said. "That's no champagne."
We drank bottles of Asti Spumante and were
having a fairly good time.
The proprietor remained sullen. Finally he
walked out.
"He probably has a mistress," Henry said. "Or
else he has gone gambling."
His wife was the cook. A small pretty woman in a
low-cut dress. Black hair, very white skin, large
dark eyes, perspiration above her top lip. She had
to finish serving the meal.
"I stayed in London with Adrian Oakes," Henry
said. "The night before flying over. He had a girl,
staying with them, that he had just before breakfast. His wife doesn't mind. It's the upper classes.
His father gave him a mistress when he was
twenty. He's been used to it since. Not like us."
When we got back we walked Fred around the
park. Ahead, in the sky, I could see Orion.
Back in the house we drank and talked about
Peter Lanyon, Patrick Heron, Terry Frost, Alan
Lowndes. And the crazy things we did.
"I remember," I said, "how we all got dressed up
in suits to go to Peter's funeral. And one of your

sons saw us walking in the street. 'You look like a bunch of gangsters,' he said."

"Who is normal?" Henry asked. "Do you know anyone who is normal? My mother's sister was called Ida Bolt. As Ida Bolt she was quiet and passive. And no one took any notice. But she also called herself Jennie Dempsey. And as Jennie Dempsey she would wiggle her hips, pretend she was dancing to the radio, jump with excitement. A complete extrovert. When she died the only people who came were those she played the piano for in a mental hospital."

Near the end he said, "There's hardly anybody left in St Ives. No one to talk to. Oh, I talk to a lot of people — but we don't go back very far."

Next morning, before seven, Henry was up. And we took Fred out for his morning walk. I have to give Fred a tennis ball so that he doesn't bark and wake up people. He gets excited as I open the door. And will leave the ball for me to throw. He doesn't wait but starts to run fast ahead. Then stops, crouches. And looks at me. When he was young, when I pitched the ball, he would catch it in his mouth. Now he misses. So I throw it over him or to one side so he can chase it. He also chases the black and grey squirrels. They always get to a tree before he can get to them. I don't think he would do anything. He just likes chasing. Then he goes off into his own world and will sniff the grass and not move for several minutes. I whistle. I call "C'mon Fred." Finally he does. Or else he goes on his back and twists his body on the grass.

Walking with Henry . . . he was noticing shapes and I was noticing colours . . . then he saw Fred was waiting for us.

"He's smiling."

"He always has that expression on his face," I said.

We went to the galleries in Yorkville. Saw some early Hans Hofmann. "I wouldn't mind having one of those," he said. At another gallery he liked the Borduas and the Riopelles. As we came out from a gallery on Scollard we came out above the street.

"There's a painting right here," he said.

I saw a red mail-box, a green metal container beside it, a cluster of three glass globes at the top of a lamp-post, a cherry tree in blossom.

"What do you look for?"

"Surfaces," he said. "That green beside the mail-box. That has a flat top. The red mail-box has a curved top. Then the cherry tree. The shape of the streetlights."

We went to the Art Gallery of Ontario. I knew some of the paintings. Van Gogh's *Woodcutters in winter*. A lovely little Renoir landscape. We go up a ramp and, on the wall, beside us, Patrick Heron's *Nude* of 1951; Peter Lanyon's *Botallack* of 1952; and Henry's *A snow day of grey* of 1953.

Henry looked pleased. "I didn't know it was here."

For lunch, in The Copenhagen, we ordered duck with red cabbage.

"Gino came to see me in Cornwall," Henry said. "I can't remember his second name. It's my memory. He was in the Italian army. In the last war. He fought on the other side. He came to see me because he likes my work. When I told him I would be in Toronto, he said to go and see a sculpture of his. Here's the envelope with the address."

In neat small writing: *Bell Canada H.Q. Trinity Square Building. Business Hours.*

We went to find it.

I don't know about Henry but I didn't expect too much. But there it was. Impressive. A tall piece of metal, with a gold coating, as a central column. And from it rods came out at right angles, as if from a spine. And these rods were close together. They went up and down the centre column. Not in a straight line but a gentle curve. And then back. The effect — when you looked at it or walked slowly around — was as if those rods were gently moving.

"Breathing," Henry said.

It went up several floors.

"It really works." Henry was delighted.

We both went to see where it had Gino's name. And what he called it. But there was no plaque, no sign, nothing to say that Gino had done it.

I asked a travel agent, on the first floor, whose door was open. She didn't know who did it. "It's just there." I asked a commissionaire on the ground floor. He didn't know.

When we left the building, to walk to the Union Station, both of us were angry.

I remembered the man in St Ives who lived down the road. A widower, in his late seventies. It

was a hot summer's day. I was coming back from
mailing some letters when he suggested I go for a
drive in the country with him.

"You could use a break."

He had a Riley. He drove up the Stennack,
turned left at the blacksmith's. And there was
Rosewall Hill with the decaying engine-houses on
the slope of moorland. He drove towards Towed-
nack. Ahead were low out-houses painted white, a
piggery. And near them, this tall brick chimney,
neatly made, tapering as it went up. Then, at the
very top, it became wider. As he drove near it, he
turned his head and said, "I did that."

After Henry left I tried to get on with some work,
but I couldn't. I phoned the hospital. My mother
was the same. As it was Sunday I decided to go for
a walk. I walked north until I came to Roselawn.
And saw fields on a residential street. They were
Jewish cemeteries. On one side were the larger
fields. Stones here had MDs and PhDs after the
names. There were several familes called Kurtz.
On one it had: "His name will live for ever." But it
was the two smaller cemeteries, on the other side
of the street, that I was drawn to. On a wooden
board, the paint fading, one had *Poland*. The other
had *Minsk*.

I sat, on the side opposite, on a green park
bench. Looked at these two small cemeteries. And
thought, this is where she belongs.

I walked back from Roselawn. Down Forest Hill Road . . . down Oriole Parkway . . . to St Clair. It had taken over an hour and as it was a warm day I sat on a bench in a small park on the corner of Avenue Road.

A few trees . . . green benches . . . I sat and smoked . . . when I noticed a sapling with a metal name-plate. I went over. *In Memory of My Beloved Papa Joseph Podobitko*. This was a good twenty minute walk from the reservoir and the little park where I lived. What was Joseph Podobitko doing here?

I phoned Sarah.

"She has stopped talking," Sarah said. "She just points with a finger. And I'm supposed to know what she wants. When I get the wrong thing, she just moves her head."

I talked to Selina.

"She's frightened of dying," Selina said. "You can see it in her eyes."

Next day I packed a white shirt, a dark tie, a suit, in case I had to stay for the funeral.

In her apartment. A feeling it's all coming to an end. The money was gone. I asked Sarah if she had taken it. She said she had.

After three days I had to return to Toronto. I went to the hospital to say goodbye. She looked thinner and smaller. But there was a youthful astonishment in her face. A luminous quality. The eyes looked very blue. She didn't have her teeth in. And the dark opening of her small mouth was in a smile.

This, I thought, is the way I want to remember her at the end. And I wanted it to end.

Weeks went by.

Selina phoned. "Why hold onto the apartment? It's paying rent for nothing."

"She needs to know she still has a place to go back to."

"She'll never go back there."

Two weeks later, Sarah phoned.

"You'll have to come and help me break it up."

"There's not much there," I said.

"I can't do it myself."

More weeks passed.

My mother started to get better. She started to take some food. Every time I now came to Ottawa another plant had died, something else was missing: the samovar, the pestle and mortar, the silver candlesticks, the silver tray, the silver coins. But she was getting stronger.

She was moved to a lower floor. They were going to try and build her up.

I dialled her number at the hospital.

"Hello," I said.

No answer.

"Hello."

"Hullo," she said, out of breath.

"How are you mother?"

"I'm fine," still out of breath. "Are you in Toronto?"

"No, I'm in Ottawa."

"In Ottawa . . . I just fell out of bed . . . to get to the phone. I'll have to call a nurse . . . I'm on the floor . . . We'll talk later."

When I went to the hospital, I asked the staff nurse where her room was. She said she would take me.

"All the nurses are fighting to look after your mother."

I wondered why.

"Because she gets all the other patients involved. She includes them in whatever she says. And she doesn't talk about herself. She doesn't turn the talk to herself."

"A doctor came to see me," my mother said, after I sat down at the end of her bed. "He was the only one who said I was not dying. That I had something. That I hadn't given up.

"You know what I get from people — respect. Some people, whatever they have on their chest, they get it out. Dinka, if she had anything she tells it. I don't. I don't tell about my husband, my children, or any of my business. They tell all. . . .

"I wish I had done something in medicine. In research."

And I remember a visit. A knock on her door. A thin elderly woman stood with her arm in a make-shift sling. "I was told to come and see you. I fell. You would know what to do." My mother examined the woman's hand, tried to move the fingers. Then announced. "Call an ambulance."

"Look what she has to read." She pointed to the books of the woman in the bed beside her who was out of the room. "Trash. You can tell she is common.

"Sarah . . . doesn't have a head. You and me we have heads."

I tried to interrupt.

"I'm not finished," she said.

"There is a little Chinese lady. I take pity on her. She can't talk English. If I go, she goes. She talks Chinese. I talk Yiddish. She has a bowl of noodles. She gets her a fork. And me a fork. And she wants us to eat out of the same bowl . . .

"A doctor who went away, on holiday, came back to see me. When he saw me he was crying. He was so pleased I was still alive.

"Where are you going? You don't have to go out.

"The Chinese lady. She is a little thing. Hardly eats. But I show her this pudding with raisins is good . . . by eating it. So then she eats. She doesn't know a word of English . . . just Chinese. But she can't walk well . . . something is wrong with her feet.

"A Polish man came up to me and began to talk in Polish. So I answered him in Polish."

"How did he know?"

"A nurse told him I came from Poland.

"Afterwards she " − indicating the bed beside her "said, I see you have a boyfriend.

"She's *prost* . . . common.

"We walk with our walkers. . . . First the little Chinese . . . then me . . . then the Polish man . . . the nurses look at us. I tell them . . . this is a masquerade . . . a cabaret. . . . They don't know whether to laugh or not."

I looked at my watch.

"What is it like outside?"

"The leaves are falling. The sun is shining. I'm going back to Toronto."

"How is the apartment?"

"Fine. I've taken my books that you have in the bedroom in the drawers."

"Good. I don't want anyone to have them."

I got up to go.

"You'll phone me tomorrow?"

"Yes. When do you finish lunch?"

"About twelve, twelve-thirty."

"I'll phone you at one."

But it was she who phoned at nine.

"I just finished breakfast."

"What did you have?"

"Juice, an egg, toast. But I couldn't eat it all. Did you have a nice time?"

"Yes, now that you're better I don't mind being here."

"What will you do with the food left in the fridge?"

"I'll give it to Mrs Tessier."

"That's good."

"Your plants . . ."

"My plans are to go back to the apartment. Will you go to the Château Laurier and get a bus to the airport?"

"No, I'll call a taxi and take a taxi to the airport."

"That's better."

"I'll write from Toronto."

Fred was the first to go. It was the end of October. A fine sunny morning. I was getting ready to take him out for what will be his last walk. He barks as he always does before he goes outside. From his bark you couldn't tell he has cancer that has spread. Fred looks up and wags his tail whenever I pat him. He is twelve and a half. It's a fine sunny day. The leaves on the ground are some of the colours of Fred, the browns. He has also white on his neck and some black on the sides, but mostly a light brown. I am waiting for the taxi to take us to the vet. Fred is sniffing the air. His head is up. His tail up and curling . . .

The next to go was Mrs Tessier.

She died in her sleep. I read her obituary in *The Citizen*. Sometimes I would see her sitting in the all-glass connecting lounge, between the buildings, with a few other ladies who lived here. They all spoke French. She always looked jolly. Her feet not touching the ground. Her husband died a few years ago. A tall nervous man with glasses. He was also quiet. They had no children. Whenever I saw her she asked, "How is your mother?"

I would tell her.

"Will she come back?"

"I don't know."

And when I was to leave the apartment early next morning for Toronto, I would knock on her door the night before and give Mrs Tessier anything perishable in the fridge. I would knock on the door and a tallish thin woman with grey hair, in a fringe, opened it apprehensively. She looked sullen. She must have been, like Mrs Tessier, in her late seventies or early eighties. Then I saw Mrs Tessier appear to the right, sideways, wrapping a dressing-gown around her. She was naked underneath. And she was wrapping the dressing-gown around as if she didn't mind being seen like this. The other lady was fully dressed.

After that, whenever I knocked, the thin sullen woman was always there, always apprehensive. Once I saw her going to Mrs Tessier's door carrying cut flowers. Sometimes when I arrived, or was leaving, I heard light laughter from behind Mrs Tessier's door. I didn't know what was going on. But I hoped they were enjoying themselves.

There was going to be a meeting with the doctor and the social worker. Sarah, Selina, and my mother would be there to decide where she would go from the hospital. I had to be in Halifax on business.

When I got back to Toronto I phoned her.

"You sound better."

"Of course," she said, "I'm eating."

"How did the meeting go?"

"You should see how mad Selina was when the doctor said if I want to go home I can try it. Oh boy, was Selina mad. She wanted me to go to some nursing home, an old age home, to an institution. Anything but to live in my home again."

"How about Sarah?"

"She said nothing."

"How do you feel?"

"I'd like to try and see if I can look after myself."

"I'll come and take you back. When will that be?"

"Next Wednesday."

"I'll come on Tuesday."

That night I spoke to Sarah on the phone. I asked about the meeting. "To get back to her place she put on some performance."

On Tuesday when I went to see her she was standing by the window with her walker watching a blizzard.

"I'll need my boots. Put on the light in the hall. I have no light in the cupboard. But you will be able to feel, at the bottom, the boots. Take a scarf from inside a sleeve from one of my coats."

When I came back next day, after lunch, she was dressed ready to go in a wheelchair.

I gave her the green and brown silk scarf. Then the boots. She put one on with difficulty. Then tried the other. It wouldn't go. She tried again. Then I tried. It only went so far.

"You brought me two right feet," she said. "How can I go like this?"

"It's not far to walk," I said. "From the taxi, over a bit of snow, to the front door of your building. You have your walker. There will be the taxi driver and me to hold you."

"Two right feet."

She thought that was very droll.

Without the samovar, or the plants, the apartment looked empty.

"It's so nice," she said. "It lights my eyes up. I feel so good. It's home."

"The plants . . ."

"It doesn't matter. This one is the healthiest. And this cutting from the rubber plant I think I can save."

She sat by the window looking at the snow-covered park. "Oh boy, Selina was mad. She wanted me to go to a nursing home. If I go to a nursing home I don't get any money from the government. This way I'll be able to leave some money to all the children.

"The sun is strong." She turned her head away from the window.

I phoned Selina at her office.

"She should be in a nursing home. I want my grandmother to live a few more years. And she will in a nursing home where they can look after her."

"She wants to be in her apartment."

"But what happens if anything goes wrong? Mummy is in Carleton Place. You are in Toronto. I'm the one who will have to look after her."

"She also said she wants to be back because of the monthly cheques."

"That's a cop-out. She doesn't want to lose her independence. That's what it's all about."

I phoned Sarah and asked if she would come and stay with mother for a while.

"I'm too tired. The place is too small. Why? Did she want me to be there?"

"No. I just wondered if you thought of it."

I asked mother, "What about having Sarah come and stay with you?"

"I don't think so. I feel better by myself."

It had rained during the night. Then it froze. On the train back to Toronto the smaller trees were bent over. Some were broken by the weight of the ice. But it all looked pretty. Mile after mile. I thought of a friend, a professor of mathematics at the University of Toronto. He has devoted his life to mathematics and to logic. I asked him, what did he make of it all.

He said. "Nothing lasts. Everything changes."

Was this why we keep making connections? Why do I connect Gino's sculpture to that tall brick chimney to those saplings with Joseph Podobitko to Mr Thomas Sachs on the door of the hospital room to those little Jewish cemeteries on Rose-lawn?

But then, whenever I go to a new place and walk around to get to know it, I inevitably end up in a cemetery.

My mother had been in her apartment a half-year when I phoned to tell her I was going to England to see my daughters. I would be away several months.

"The children have to know they have a father," she said.

I told her I would come tomorrow. "I'll see you around one-fifteen.

"Any time. You will be a good guest."

She had put on weight, and now could walk without a walker. But she still looked frail.

The place looked clean. The two surviving plants looked healthy. But without the samovar it seemed empty.

"Selina has it in the basement," she said. "What is a samovar doing in a basement?"

She wanted to make tea. And did, taking her time. I brought in the cups and saucers. She brought in the teapot.

"When I came home . . . everything was dirty —
the dishes.

"Not any more the people who used to be — the
apartments are empty."

She talked about Mrs Tessier.

"People in the building told me because I wasn't
in my apartment Mrs Tessier couldn't go to sleep."

"How often do you go to the hospital?"

"Once every two weeks. When the doctor looks
at me — the big smile. He is so happy. "If I was in a
nursing home I would be dead."

She left the table and disappeared into the
bedroom. Came back with several twenty-dollar
bills. Put them in my hands.

"For the children."

She sat down, slowly, by the table. "You know
the money I was saving for a trip to England."

We were silent.

"Only another seven years and you will get the
old age pension. That's wonderful," she said. And
began to take out her hearing aid. Then put it back
in. "It should make a noise if it is working." I tried a
new battery. It still wasn't working. She finally
gave up and said she would get the nurse tomorrow to find out about it.

After that it was difficult to have a conversation.
There were silences.

"Did you watch *Shoah* on television?"

She didn't answer. I didn't know if she heard.

"It's about European Jews being taken to concentration camps in Poland."

"No," she said quietly. "I watch *Guiding Light*
and *The Young and the Restless*."

I must have looked puzzled.
"It's soap," she said, raising her voice.
I said nothing.
"It's soap opera," she said loudly.
And she was angry.